MW01535728

WHISPERS OF DANGER AND LOVE

JANIS LANE

SOUL MATE PUBLISHING

New York

WHISPERS OF DANGER AND LOVE

Copyright©2016

JANIS LANE

Cover Design by Melody A. Pond

This book is a work of fiction. The names, characters, places, and incidents are the products of the author's imagination or are used fictitiously. Any resemblance to actual events, business establishments, locales, or persons, living or dead, is entirely coincidental.

Published in the United States of America by
Soul Mate Publishing
P.O. Box 24
Macedon, New York, 14502

ISBN: 978-1-68291-167-9

ebook ISBN: 978-1-68291-140-2

www.SoulMatePublishing.com

Yes, in the poor man's garden grow

Far more than herbs and flowers-

Kind thoughts, contentment, peace of mind,

And joy for weary hours.

—Mary Howett, "The Poor Man's Garden"

Dedicated to gardeners the wold over

and to those who love them.

May your life be filled with sunshine,

enough rain to make your garden grow,

and a few weeds to keep you humble.

—EJLane

Chapter 1

Testosterone surged as six half-naked men sped around the backyard, slapping the ball with grunts of satisfaction followed by abject moans of despair when they missed. Well-developed muscles glistened with sweat as they rippled.

Detective David Larkin, enjoying a late summer day off, would not admit to fatigue. Early thirties was not too old to play a rousing game of volleyball. Hoping to end the game, he gave an overhead slam all he had. At the last minute, his foot slipped in the long grass, causing him to pull back.

The ball flew to one side, hit the post, and arched high, clearing the tall hedge which separated the backyard from the property next door. The men stopped, stock-still, gazing with grinning faces as the ball hung suspended in the air momentarily before it started its downward swing. A couple of "wahoos" and some light applause provided sound effects. Shortly after the ball disappeared from view, a shrill, panicked scream pierced the air.

Larkin, assuming responsibility, trotted over and thrust his head through the dense foliage, earning him a long scratch down one grizzled chin.

A trim, rounded bottom and a better-than-average pair of decidedly feminine long legs, short shorts, and bare feet captured his attention as he frantically scanned the area. Her head hidden from his view, the noisy creature sobbed as she bent over the flower garden in front of her.

Oh Lordy! *Did the volleyball harm a pet?* David tried to push his shoulders through the hedge. It may have been the only time in his life he regretted the width. While he struggled, his neighbor shouted angrily at him.

"Larkin! Do you see what you've done, you clumsily beast?"

He struggled to follow her fingers pointing at the ground. Her face was red, and he imagined waves of fury escaping from the top of her pretty head.

He actually couldn't see, although he spotted a reddish-purple lump at the base of those bare toes. *Was something bleeding?* A surge of adrenaline gave his pulse a jump, and he struggled with the hedge a moment more before he gave up and pulled himself back through. He ran a few steps toward the back where he remembered a narrow opening. A quick sideways thrust gained entry to the garden next door.

"Did I hurt your little dog, Cher?"

He reached the side of the curly haired brunette and stared down at the carnage.

"This is yours." She picked up the volleyball gingerly with fingertips and shoved it in his face. "I do not own a dog. I have never owned a dog. Dogs dig up gardens," she said, ice dripping from a pair of lips that would have been inviting had they not been stretched thin over clenched teeth.

David clasped the ball between his hands. Even he could appreciate the odiferous fumes wafting from the well-used volleyball, now with a dark red smear on one side. He didn't think it was blood.

"I'm sorry," he said, even as he appraised with interest the trim figure bristling in front of him. "What did I hit?" He tried without success to peer around her at the lump. All he could see was a drawing tablet with a sketch teetering on the edge of a folding table. A plant, perhaps? Had he crushed a plant of some sort?

"This lily, now ruined for the rest of the season"—she paused and pointed for emphasis—"is a one-of-a-kind." She caught her breath and shuddered before rushing on. "It's a new kind of lily. It is so new there is no name for it as yet."

David relaxed. It wasn't a pet, but only some old plant. What an alarmist! The same old Cher, always making a fuss. Those screams had sounded seriously like something critical. He'd been on the verge of dialing 911 and had made ready to initiate first aid. He'd just had a refresher course. His superior, Detective Kevin Fowler, had insisted all the staff stay current, but he was pleased he didn't need to use it today.

"I'm sorry about your plant, hon. Lucky someone wasn't hurt." He patted her awkwardly on the nearest shoulder, which she jerked angrily away. She turned her back to him and took a step.

Noise from the hedge caught his attention and he laughed to see heads popping through the foliage. The scene resembled some crazy carnival game of disjointed heads.

One of his buddies, a broad grin on his face and his head stuck through the hedge called out, "Hey, Dave. I gotta go. See you next week, and we'll finish the game." Two other heads, which had popped through the thick foliage, presented faces that sparkled with delight when they spotted the attractive woman with the thunderous expression.

"Oh-oh. Got your hands full now, Dave. Think you can handle that all by yourself? Go easy, now, big fellow. We don't want anyone hurt."

"Sure you don't need company over there?"

"Might as well call the game. Looks like you got some fixing up to do, ole buddy. See you next week." The heads popped back through the hedge, and David turned to his neighbor.

"Been a long time, Cher. I guess you know I just moved into my grandmother's house." He grinned at her while he twirled the volleyball up and down. How grownup she appeared from the last time he had seen her. How many years had it been? Obviously too long! He hadn't remembered those long legs. The rest of her wasn't bad either, in spite of the unfriendly expression she telegraphed. He had to restrain himself from reaching over and giving her the big bear hug he longed to do.

She stared up at him through narrowed eyes. "Yes, and the several years I lived next door to that lovely lady, never once did a prize lily get destroyed by a flying anything!" She turned her back to him again and knelt with a sorrowful expression beside the crushed blossom.

He glanced again at the sketchpad to see what it might have looked like before his fateful overhead smash. A lily wasn't all that special. It shouldn't be difficult to find another. He shrugged. "Well, I gotta go and get cleaned up. I really am sorry about your posy, but it's nice to see you again after all this time." He flashed her his famous, winsome grin guaranteed to tempt even the most truculent conquest to his side. He received a stony glare in return.

Okay. Obviously she was still angry. He might need to work a bit on this one; buy her a bouquet of flowers or something. Chocolate, they all like chocolate anything. He gave her a half salute while she stared coldly over her shoulder at him. He trotted down the hedge line and disappeared through the pass through.

After her new neighbor left, Cheryl tried to settle back to her work. Her column wouldn't write itself and she respected the deadline.

The "Right Way" to Garden
by Cheryl

Frequently I am asked to discuss the "right way" to garden, which is a tough question for me to answer. Actually, in my opinion, there is no such thing as a "right way." There is only what makes the gardener happy with her/his efforts, with the caveat, of course, that your neighbors haven't called the zoning board of appeals to complain, or all the plants haven't died from lack of attention to the placement.

"Total Beast! Always been a beast, is still a beast," Cher spit out between tightly clamped jaws, feeling a vein throb in her forehead. She took a deep breath trying valiantly to regain her composure and still her racing pulse. A moment ago, she was content in her peaceful garden sketching an exciting new specimen. Now her blood pressure must be off the scale and her temper set on boil. The unexpected appearance of David Larkin had caught her completely unaware. Sure, she had heard the noise from next door and regretted the absence of her lovely older neighbor, who shared her love of gardening, but she hadn't thought to be confronted by his presence so soon.

"Why did I think he would sell the house? Should've known he would cause the maximum of confusion. Always did, always will." Cheryl scanned the border of her blazing, full-bloom perennial flowerbeds. The sight usually gave her a feeling of pleasure and a sense of accomplishment. Her nerves slowly settled and finally she turned back to her laptop.

Take the perennial, Anthemis, a pretty butter-*yellow daisy, for example. The more you love it, tend it, pamper it, the less successful you will become. This plant thrives on neglect and is a perfect choice for a casual approach to gardening. So one of the first questions I usually ask a client is how much time does the gardener intend to spend "hands on" with her/his plants.*

Cheryl tried without success to thrust aside the vision of a broad-shouldered, naked chest of a brute of a male with an untidy thatch of coal-black hair falling into his face, as he invaded her garden, bringing with him his usual chaos. Her garden column had to be completed by this afternoon and emailed before five. She was acutely regretting that she had left it until the last minute, but she hadn't wanted to wait another day to sketch the long-awaited bloom of the cultivated hybrid lily. Surging fury tightened her throat at the sight of the crushed petals. She had so carefully tended the cultivation of this bulb. A two-year project was just now coming to an end. A glimpse only of the gorgeous bloom, and smash, it was over.

Who cared how handsome he was? Those shoulders could have been on a wrestler, but who wanted a sports jock for a neighbor? She was still grieving for the gracious lady from next door who had shared her passion for gardening. What kind of grandson never visited his grandmother?

One lady I know works full time, volunteers in several worthwhile charities, and is—with her husband—raising two healthy children. She also has a love of gardening. Her backyard is a showpiece of colorful elegance. How does she accomplish this, which, I might add, she does with grace and talent? The answer is easy: Her garden is tightly organized.

From experience, she knows which plants grow best and where. Out her back door and off her deck she designated a three-by-four-foot plot for brightly colored annuals. Visible from her breakfast table, this tightly contained garden adds to the enjoyment of her first cup of coffee every morning. Spikes of Rocket snapdragons bloom with a ring of white, sweet alyssum. For variety, she might change the type of annuals each year.

"Always breaking my things," Cheryl fumed with her head whirling with unbidden memories. She stomped her foot. "Who was it who broke my best tea set? Who teased Nana's parrot until it squawked every time he came near?

"Beast! Why, oh why, couldn't a nice family with sweet little girls move in next door?" she moaned aloud. She leaned over and petulantly yanked a weed up by the roots and shook it hard. Soil flew everywhere, including in her face and on her blouse.

Two baskets of pansies in one lightly shaded corner are still merrily smiling with their blotched faces. At the end of the season, after the first frost, this prepared lady pulls up and discards the colorful annuals, gives the bed a quick mulch, and then adds whimsical statuary to mark the spot. Snow soon gives the bed a seasonal cover, but the tall statue adds winter interest.

"I swear, if he starts aggravating me . . ." Cher paused, trying to calm herself, and then continued.

The rest of the yard? On the deck, a new variety of dwarf blueberries thrive in good-sized, decorative urns to mark one side of a picnic table complete with a brightly stripped umbrella. Not only did the short shrubs sport attractive foliage but produced edible berries in summer and showy red leaves in the fall.

After trying, without much success, to put her anger to one side, Cheryl stood and paced to the mailbox and back. "He hung my doll with my jump rope. Broke my skates with his big, beastie feet." Then she resettled, her fingers on the keyboard of her laptop.

More potted plants were located strategically around the yard where container gardening was used to good advantage. While the various pots needed to be watered frequently—a chore she hired out to her teenagers for a raise in their allowances—there was almost zero need for weeding. Controlled, almost a minimalist approach, would be a name for this type of gardening. It works well for her, fits into her time schedule and her need to enjoy a growing bright spot here and there. This lady is a gardener. She has found a way for her garden to match her lifestyle.

Cheryl paused when she heard the tinkle of a bell toward the front of her cottage. It was late in the day for a customer, but there hadn't been many lately. She ended the column with a promise to discuss a different type of gardening for next week, closed her laptop with a snap, and ran toward the front door. It was not smart to ignore potential customers. A hurried peek at her curls and a swipe toward a smear of dirt on one cheek, and she was through the hall and into what once was a living room, now remodeled into a compact gardening shop.

"Hi. I'm here to make amends." Looming, shutting out the light, Brute the Lily Killer, stood filling the room with his beastly body full of rippling muscles and a smattering of black chest hair peeking from the neck of his red polo shirt. Streaks from a comb through his thick, black hair hinted it was still wet from his shower. It wasn't raining. He was several inches taller than her five-foot-five. She had to look up at him while he directed an—she knew it had to be fake—apologetic eye back down at her. He had rich brown eyes with golden flecks, long curly lashes. She re-tagged him a browned-eyed Giant Lily Killer.

From behind his back, he brought three hothouse roses and held them forward. Over in the corner, a large red parrot paced uneasily back and forth on its perch.

"Ack! Naughty boy! Naughty boy!" The parrot squawked and ruffled its feathers.

Larkin spotted the bird and smiled boldly. "I really am sorry I squished your plant, but I'm glad it wasn't more serious." He eyed the parrot. "Pretty Polly, want a cracker?" Larkin asked in a singsong, teasing voice.

The bird left its perch and flew with flapping wings into its nearby cage. With his sharp bill, it plucked the door shut with a snap, turning its head to one side to eye the detective closely.

Cheryl took the three stems, gave them a cursory glance, and shook them in his face. "You obviously have no idea what is and what isn't serious to me. If you knew more about me, you would never purchase these soulless roses with no fragrance, imported from who knows where, and sprayed with God-knows-what."

She glared at him. "This is my livelihood, I'll have you know. This is my shop, my business. I'm a gardening consultant and my plants are precious to me."

He backed up a step in the face of her fury but the grin remained intact.

"I do not play ball in my backyard. Your grandmother would be upset if she knew you were wrecking her gorgeous flowerbeds." She paused and took a deep breath. His half-grin revealed flashes of white teeth, and somewhere deep inside she acknowledged a need to answer that smile. Rigorously she suppressed it. "It's obvious you have no idea of the seriousness of your actions."

"But, Cher!" His grin disappeared while his face segued into a true study in consternation. She hid a smile at the expression on his wicked, albeit too handsome, pirate face. He curled his hand around the battered and scentless roses as she turned to leave the room.

"Cher. Don't you even have a hug for me for old time's sake?"

She turned and pointed at a stack of business cards in a holder sitting on the counter.

"I'm in the book. Not that you'll ever need to discuss how to improve your backyard, but that's my business." With that parting shot, she disappeared into the back of the shop leaving him standing with his giant, plant-killer mouth hanging wide open.

Contrast this with a fellow who is spending his retirement years working in his two-acre yard. From early morning he can be found in his perennial garden, which covers a goodly portion of his acreage. Groups asked for tours, and garden clubs haunted him for names of plants until he wrote discreet labels. His life is gardening. He is content and intends to spend the rest of his life doing exactly what he did the year before, working laboriously in his garden. You start to see my point?

These two examples and everything in-between is the "right way" to garden. If you like it, it makes you happy, and the neighbors aren't too upset, then it's the right way to garden. Personality tests are not necessary before I recommend a planting design, but I do insist we sit chatting for a bit. It is my belief a successful garden means the plants fit the person's lifestyle and personality and vice versa. A happy customer in a thriving garden is the measure of my success. Happy Gardening,

Cheryl

Cheryl snapped the top of her laptop closed. "Whew. Finally finished for the week." She paused before leaving the garden to hear banging and the alarming sound of metal on metal penetrating through the hedge from next door. She tilted her chin up on her way inside, refusing to allow her peace to be disturbed by a shallow, albeit Rhett Butler handsome, beast of a destroyer of delicate things. Oh, if only he had the manners of a southern gentleman. She was certain Scarlet never had to put up with such Neanderthal tactics.

Her cell rang. When she flipped it open and recognized the number, she snapped it shut again. An ex-fiancé was not on her list of need-to-tend-to today. Men were beginning to be not on her list of important items, if it came to that.

David Larkin was enough of a disturbance in her life without adding the nuisance of an ex-boyfriend, doctor or not. Her parents, no, her mother, still held out hope she would change her mind about Gordon Moore, but Cheryl knew there was no chance she would. She had broken the engagement over a year ago. Why he kept calling, she could not understand. By now he must realize how serious she was about her occupation. She had settled into her new life and obviously he was upset that it didn't include him. What he wanted with a lady who was happiest when she had soil underneath her fingernails, she couldn't imagine.

Those long idyllic days spent in her grandmother's presence had had a profound influence on a young Cheryl. She still owned her first pair of gardening gloves and trowel given her by that sweet lady. Side by side, they dug and planted in the languid summer days and long twilights, turning the yard into a blazing place of color and fragrance, alive with bees, birds, and butterflies. Cheryl loved the peace and contentment she found there and the sweet memory of a wonderful grandmother who had time for her.

Her mother had been and still was a busy woman filling her days with charity work and country club activities. Leaving Cheryl with her grandmother had been both a convenience and a delight to a lonely child. First peeking through the hedge with curiosity and spying a noisy boy, Cheryl had found herself astounded at his rowdy behavior. He became a fascination. She had followed him around, eyes wide with delight and amazement in the excitement he created. Her grandmother frowned and said he needed the seat of his pants warmed but added that he might be interesting in a few years if he managed to grow up. Judging from the fate of her prized lily, Cheryl wondered if David had managed that task yet. He was much too old to have the seat of his pants warmed, wasn't he?

Chapter 2

Notes and Ideas for future columns:
A) Gardening is a work in progress. There's no such thing as perfect and complete. Perfectly completed gardens might be made from silk.

Flat out B) desirable C) least desirable D) Politically correct E) compromise

How to eat your—green—way through your flowerbed and still pick bouquets in the morning.

A) Parsley border B) salad greens in the corner C) blueberry bushes turn red, beans on a trellis D) tea garden to share with the bees and butterflies.

Get this emailed off to Beverly Hampton soon. Do not delay.

Cheryl unlocked the front door of her shop and stood happily sniffing a mild breeze which fluttered the petals in her front garden, now in colorful mid-summer riot. Bees buzzed working each plant seriously for nectar, while sulfur-yellow butterflies flitted from flower to flower sipping delicately, then dashing away to find another blossom. She loved how they flew in zigzagging patterns around the yard. Probably an innate tactic to avoid capture, but it always made Cheryl smile.

She gazed up and down the street spotting neither car nor person. It was usually quiet on this side street which was slowly changing from residential to business. The town of Hubbard, New York, which started out as an independent community had grown and grown until it was now considered a bedroom village to a larger city. It still contained the remains of a native population, the offspring of the original settlers, who determined to keep the village atmosphere intact.

Usually a safe and pleasant address to own, Cheryl was pleased to call it home. Her grandmother's modest cottage was loved and familiar, providing her both a home and a place for her budding business. She laughed at her accidental pun.

She could have joined her father in business. She had an impressive degree which proclaimed she was imminently qualified. Almost. Something nudged her into entering school once more and, in spite of her mother's objection, she obtained a degree in horticulture and landscaping.

Her bewildered father attempted to be supportive when she took the deed from her grandmother and opened her little shop. To give him credit, he had never chastised her for her decision not to join him, although she guessed how disappointed he must be. Regretful for upsetting her parents, she was nevertheless surprised but pleased at just how sublimely happy she was. It had been a tough decision, not to mention a bit scary, but it was done, and she was grateful it seemed to be the right one.

A healthy trust fund from her parents and this cottage left to her from her beloved grandmother allowed her to operate a business doing what she loved best. Fortunately, she snagged extra money writing a garden column suggested by her friend, Beverly Hampton, editor of the local newspaper. Would she have time to complete a manuscript on her version of gardening? She hoped so. It was in her long-range plans, and Beverly had encouraged her to work on it.

Cheryl hadn't had anything in her budget for advertising. Mostly her clients were recommended to her by word of mouth. A satisfied customer is always the best advertisement, she thought happily as the phone rang inside the shop.

She made an appointment later in the day to discuss what could turn out to be a highly lucrative job. Hands on work was not her plan. She wouldn't do the work herself. No, she would interview the client, scope out the garden, and then make recommendations. Often she merely helped a new gardener identify the plants already growing in the yard of an older home, guiding young couples who were at loss when confronted by a yard full of established plants. Soon, hopefully, they would feel comfortable enough to branch out and make it their own. It was one of her most favorite tasks in this business of gardening. Her goal was to instill a love for plants to all who sought her work.

Sam Toledo. Where had she heard that name before? She wrote his name in her appointment book before sitting down to do a bit of work. Deeply absorbed in acquainting herself with the growing habits of a new variety of Echinacea, she was startled when the little bell on the shop door dinged, the light dimmed, and she looked up once more into the dark-brown eyes of her next-door neighbor. The fragrance of his spicy shaving lotion tickled her nose as she frowned at him.

The parrot squawked, "Naughty Boy," and paced back and forth on his perch.

Larkin grinned and saluted the bird.

"I brought you an éclair, little Cher," he announced, pulling a chair closer, sitting down and thrusting a paper bag onto her desktop.

Darn, why must he remember her weakness? At least it wasn't more commercial flower bouquets. Perhaps he was finally remembering her actual identity. Probably not though. That would require more sensitivity than David Larkin could produce in one day.

"Don't you work for a living?" she asked, trying in vain to resist opening the bag, gave up, and reached greedily for the chocolate-covered, calorie-laden pastry. She took a huge bite and sighed with pleasure as the rich vanilla pudding squished inside her mouth with sinful goodness.

"I'm on a case. You haven't yet appreciated that I'm now a full-fledged detective. That's an important position in the police department, I'll have you know. You should show me more respect. Hubbard is still a little town, but it's growing and, fortunately for me, they've decided to hire more policemen." He thrust both shoes on the edge of her desk and tilted back in his chair.

"Oh, sure. What are you investigating? Éclairs? Tell the truth. You've come to destroy another of my plants. Confess. You'll feel much better when you admit to your sins." The last word became garbled on a huge bite of the éclair and she almost choked. He jumped to pound her on the back while she waved her hands to stop him. Gasping, she glared at him, even more furious when she spotted that predatory gleam in his eye.

"I'm sorry about your posy, honey. You know I'd never hurt anything of yours unless it was an accident."

It was such an outrageous lie she could only stare at the man who had given her grief since she was ten years old.

"You know all those other times were pure accidents," he continued with perfect composure, reaching over to tweak a curl that had fallen over her forehead. "Cute haircut, but I liked it better when it was in braids."

She opened her mouth to argue.

"Come on, Cher. Let's be friends," he said, a soft, sultry change slipping easily into his voice.

She assigned the Italian part of David to this voice. Naming off various countries he could claim as a partial birthright, he had called his heritage as jumbled as a junkyard dog. Cheryl had assigned personality traits to each one. Sexy was Italian.

"Grandma left me the house and I guess yours did too. Neighbors again. Did you miss me all these years?" He gazed around him at the tidy little shop. "I see you inherited Polly parrot. How old is she now?" He eyed a monitor in the corner which was flipping colorful gardening scenes one after another.

"This is nice," he said. "When did you decide to open a shop? I thought you were off getting another degree in something or other." He turned back to her with a friendly half-smile masquerading this time as a normal American next-door neighbor. It was here that Cheryl was most susceptible. She sat up with a wary eye, swallowed, and resisted another bite.

"I finished my degrees a few years ago when you were off playing soldier. Time has passed you by, David. You should have visited your grandmother more often. She would have kept you up on all the doings of the Esterbrooks." Cheryl leaned over and shut the ornate birdcage, hoping the parrot would stay quiet. There was a clear animosity between David Larkin and the bird, whose memory documented well-deserved and long-held grievances.

"I know," David agreed, ruffling his hair restlessly. "I meant to, but life got complicated and I kept putting it off. I'm sorry now. I miss her and feel guilty every time I think about how long it was since I visited." He gazed out the window at the hedge separating the two dwellings.

"I was shocked when she left me the house, you know." She guessed from the tone of his voice he was serious. He really meant it. Was this the Scot or the Irish piece he used to express his guilt?

"She used to talk about you all the time. She kept up with your doings over the years, although she didn't care much for your lady friends." Cheryl glanced at him from underneath her eyelashes.

His eyes twinkled but his face transformed into inscrutably bland nothingness. She snorted, and he flashed a broad grin. She struggled to maintain her composure albeit recognizing the memorial power of that smile. There was history between the two of them. For a moment, the years dropped away, and two naughty children sat together plotting their next wicked escapade.

Abruptly, he dropped his feet and jerked a buzzing cell from his pocket. As he barked his name into the receiver, she watched, fascinated, while he completed a metamorphosis from her old nemeses into a cop. Hard planes appeared on his cheeks, his lips thinned, and his eyes narrowed then went flat. Belatedly she noticed the butt of a gun riding in a shoulder hostler underneath his loose jacket. His conversation consisted of one-word answers, grunts, and short questions. Cheryl could draw no conclusions, but her curiosity was alive and well. This must be the stern German part of David at work.

"Gotta go, sweet thing." He leaned over, grabbed the nape of her neck, and, taking advantage of her astonished mouth dropping open, kissed her hard with a quick thrust of his tongue. One rough finger tilted her chin up as he looked deep into her eyes for a nano second, and then chuckled deep in his throat. The Italian Stallion was back.

"Yum, like honey nectar, still sweet Cher," he murmured.

She felt her mouth gaping like the Grand Canyon as he walked swiftly out the door. Good Lord. After all these years, you'd think she would be prepared for his outrageous behavior. But she never was. It was part of the pathology of their relationship that he could shock her senseless—every single time, over and over.

Waiting for the tingling to stop, Cheryl sat rubbing her lips as she watched a beat-up, plain-brown-wrapper automobile, lights flashing on the dash board, peel out of the drive way next door. Drawing deep breaths in and out, she grabbed her stomach and tried to quiet her pounding pulse. She hadn't had a reaction like that since the beastly Lily Killer had stepped in and ruined her high school prom.

"I will not allow him to come back into my life. I swear on my best boots I will control myself. I don't know how he manages to seduce me like that. When will I ever learn?"

Over in the corner, her parrot squawked in a facsimile of her grandmother's voice, "Ack! Naughty Boy!"

"You got that right, Ganymede. He's been a naughty boy all his life!"

Cheryl stalked out to the garden and calmed herself by furiously weeding a perennial bed. A tiny Sphinx Moth buzzed her ear and settled in a patch of impatiens nearby. The soft sounds soothed her as the tiny humming bird look-alike drew sweet nectar from the blossoms. She settled back on her heels to watch. Bees and colorful butterflies flitted throughout the garden filled with peak July blooms. A gloriously red cardinal, almost like a flower himself, was stridently singing, warning other males to stay out of his territory. She allowed her mind to wander, her eyes unfocused while her thoughts strayed to her childhood.

David Larkin was four years older than she. What did that make him now? Thirty-three and a half? Living all their lives next door to each other, their grandmothers had been friends. Frequently Cheryl would find David playing in the backyard when she came to spend time with her Nana. He'd fascinated a lonely little girl with no siblings with his merry grin and a winning way of presenting "the plan" for the day to little next-door Gullible Cheryl. She would fall into helping him build a tree house in his Granny's best fruit tree, allow him to haul up her best toy tea set which he promptly smashed in some sort of gravity experiment. A beloved doll served as a hung pirate while he stalked her with a sword made from a cardboard paper roll.

His laughter proved contagious, his antics irresistible, and she followed him like a faithful puppy in and out of scrapes which grew worse each year that passed. David Larkin, the Pied Piper of the neighborhood. But as she entered high school, he disappeared from the scene and there were four blessed years of trouble free visits. She was growing up and not as interested in boisterous games with a rough boy. Her grandmother said he was away from home.

In high school, she developed a super crush on a hulking football player. She was thrilled when he asked her to the prom and felt sophisticated in her strapless gown as they headed to someone's post prom house. The party was wild, the music was loud, and some kids were drinking. There weren't many students there that she knew, but she was excited to be included. Her new strapless prom dress, a mass of row upon row of delicate blue ruffles and almost the most perfect dress she had ever owned, seemed to be of great interest to her date. He kept rubbing her arm and accidentally dragging her bodice down bit by bit. She tugged it back up, and he would rub it back down. He didn't appear as cute as she once thought.

Eventually it dawned on her the party was without chaperones, although there did seem to be several young adults present. When she commented on this fact, her date smirked and invited her for a walk out by the pool where he steered her toward a pool house, a cabana of sorts. As the door opened, she had a sudden premonition she didn't belong there and started to pull away.

"Oh no, you don't," her date said, laughing and grasping her arm painfully.

She caught a strong odor of some sort of liquor on his breath, although as far as she knew only a fruit punch had been served.

"You don't flake out on me now," he uttered in her ear with a threatening leer. He gave her a quick shove, and she flew through the door and fell onto a lounge chair. She was grabbing at the aggravating bodice of her strapless gown when he climbed on top of her, smothering her with unwanted kisses. She pushed at his arms, but he seemed to be all octopus. And then it happened. The memory of that night could still cause her pulse to throb with shock.

She had heard a warrior's whoop, and her date suddenly flew through the air and landed on his butt with a surprised *oomph*.

David Larkin stood over him with his fist raised and a fierce scowl on his handsome face. Was he Jack Sparrow or Tarzan that night? David leaned down and jerked her obnoxious date up by the front of his tux, and then, with his other hand on the seat of the boy's pants, he duck-walked the cowering young man out the door.

Cheryl had been too surprised to react. She jumped up, tugging at her bodice, and ran outside after them in time to see her date disappearing into the distance.

"What did you do!" she screamed at Larkin who stood grinning down at her, his tousled, thick, black hair needing a cut and spilling forward. His chin was covered with a thin bearded growth giving him a rough, ultra-male appearance. She was even more furious at the rapid beat of her betraying heart when he moved closer and touched her cheek, caressing it with a fingertip.

"Don't you look pretty, sweet little thing." He tipped her chin up and gave her a gentle kiss on the lips. Before she could utter a strongly worded protest, he hustled her toward the street and escorted her into a red pick-up truck, tucking her long dress in afterward. German Gestapo, beast, bully.

"Time you were in bed, little girl. Don't think you'll miss that goon. I'll just see you home." David had buckled her seat belt and given a satisfied pat to her leg pausing momentarily to caress the silky material. "Nice," he had murmured.

Firmly closing the door, he rounded the cab, climbed into the driver's seat, and revved the engine. "Hold on, honey," he whispered, flashing those strong, super-white teeth at her. He stepped briskly on the accelerator.

"David Larkin, have you lost your mind? What did you do to my date? This is my high school prom, I'll have you know. You are not welcome to . . . Where have you been? You can't just suddenly appear and act as if you think you are my father. David! What are you doing?"

She argued and stomped her feet, but he just grinned and drove straight to her house. He walked her to the door and stood looking down at her in the dim glow of a distant streetlight. Spring breezes caressed her shoulders as she stared up at him.

"Pretty little Cher. So sweet. You're almost grown up, aren't you? When did that happen?" He tilted her chin up firmly with one hand reaching behind to hold her head with the other. His lips were firm, warm and he uttered a low groan. His arms came around her as he pulled her close, snuggling her firmly against his lanky length, and deepening the kiss. His tongue probed between her lips which parted as if he had taken control away from her. She gasped as his tongue flicked in and out causing alarming sensations in her stomach and sliding down her torso to other warm places. When she thought she would die from the pleasure, he pulled abruptly away.

"David!" she said, reaching up to touch her lips.

He grinned and flashed his strong, white teeth at her. He was a pirate from the far-off seas come to kidnap her with her a willing prisoner. Her head reeled from the excitement.

"Sorry, honey. Didn't mean for that to happen. You just smelled so good I lost it for a bit. Say hello to your mama and daddy for me. Don't grow up too fast. Night, night, sweets." Whistling merrily, David turned and headed toward his truck, giving her a quick salute before he disappeared into the night.

She stood on the steps fingering her wrist corsage, staring at the quickly disappearing taillights of his truck until it turned the corner and was gone. The shock of the night was almost gone as her head was filled only with a kiss from bad boy David Larkin.

It was all over school the next day that she'd been too chicken to stay with her date. Suffering the painful embarrassment only a teenager could feel, she thought she would never forgive David Larkin, but over time, she came to understand he had done her a favor. And she would have likely been assaulted had David not come to her rescue. Her crush on an idiotic football player had ended that night. She'd never confessed it, but she never forgot David's kiss either. It'd far surpassed the one he had given her on her thirteenth birthday when he laughed and declared he would be the first boy to kiss her.

A louder hum grazed her face and a real hummingbird, a male, his chest blazing an announcement of his ruby-throated name, scolded her for blocking his attempt to sample the nectar of a late columbine. Coming back to the present, she stood, still touching her lips and vowing never to allow Larkin to know he affected her that deeply. It would be a disastrous mistake, and she knew it.

His reputation preceded him. A string of females with various reputations had no doubt enjoyed that super-sized kiss, and she could be nothing special to him. Her head would rule her heart this time. She trailed her fingers gently against a bed of fragrant sky-blue petunias as she found her way back inside. She had work to do and an appointment in an hour or so. Besides, she was too old to have her wits scattered by a kiss from a casual acquaintance. Tell that to my unruly libido, she thought with a sinking heart.

Chapter 3

"I just love those blue flowers. I had the decorator put my new blue couch right up against the window. Could I pick these kinds of flowers and put them there?" The blond woman reached her hand down to fondle a blossom, crushing it between her fingers, and then rubbing them on her sleeve. The sap of a petunia was sticky.

It seemed strange to Cheryl why so many people would touch a plant and then deliberately destroy it by crushing or rubbing the leaves until they turned brown. Some sort of claiming possession? As often as she could she tried to teach the uninitiated how to 'pet' a plant without harming it.

"You certainly can pick bouquets when we get you a cutting garden established. Those particular plants would probably not make good arrangements. Petunias have floppy, short stems which makes them difficult to handle in a vase. Let me show you some examples of good cut flowers."

Cheryl led the buxom blonde through the garden to the back where she had planted a particular bed, an abundance of suitable cut flowers. Zinnias, gladiola, and phlox were in full mid-summer riot. A bed of Asiatic lilies were almost finished.

"Now, these zinnias come in many colors, and you can pick them to your heart's content. Aren't they pretty?" Cheryl rested her hand casually on one fiery red bloom with pride.

"Well, yeah, but I liked the blue ones best. The man at the store said my color blue was called cerulean blue. So exciting. It had a shiny finish with these cute little knobby things sticking out. Just exactly the color of those other flowers. How come these don't come in blue?" The woman stuck out her lower lip and, to Cheryl's surprise, actually pouted.

"Don't get your bowels in an uproar, doll. She'll get you some blue ones, won't you, Miss Esterbrook?" Sam Toledo snuggled his arm comfortingly around his blond friend and gave her a swift hug. Doll looked at him adoringly and patted him on his bushy head, the rings on her fingers catching the rays of the sun and practically blinding Cheryl. The blonde's other arm clutched a pink silk bag from which peeked an insignificant bug-eyed dog. At first Cheryl thought it was a stuffed animal until it gave a wheezy cough and shuddered.

Was the puppy cold? He seemed to be either terrified or freezing. Since the temperature outside was reading in the low 80's she surmised it was the former.

"Pooky here just loves blue flowers," Doll cooed.

Cheryl wasn't certain whether Pooky was the boyfriend or the dog. The dog gave a tiny spasmodic bark, and Doll giggled and covered him with kisses. She seemed particularly pleased when its tongue enthusiastically licked her mouth.

Sam Toledo wandered back toward the front of the shop lighting a pungent-smelling cigar as he walked. A stocky man, he was at least a head shorter than his companion. His shoulders were wide as if to compensate for his lack of height. A raspy voice seemed to belong to the rough face which sported a scar on one cheek, a broken nose, and a swath of reddish hair. Cheryl was startled by the beefy size of his hands. Had he been a boxer?

He bit off the tip of the cigar and spit it over into her prize red crocosmias, startling a female hummer who was feasting on the graceful arch of blooms. Cheryl made a mental note to find it later. The only thing more obnoxious than a smoker was one who butted his leftovers into her plants. Her attention was drawn back to Doll, who had tucked her puppy back into his bag.

"Lovey says you'll come right out to the house and help our gardener. How soon can you be there? I want it all finished in two weeks." She waved her hand to flash her huge diamonds for emphasis.

Cheryl presumed 'Lovely' to be Sam Toledo. So Pooky, the dog, Lovey Toledo, and Doll, the woman. Perhaps soon she could acquire more formal names. She certainly hoped so.

"We're having a big party, lots of very important people coming. I promised Lovey I would have everything shipshape by then. And I want to have a big bouquet of blue flowers for my vases. You can fix that, can't you? My friend, Sally, said you can work wonders in the garden. Can you?" A shrewd expression flitted over her face and a hard look came into the blonde's eyes for a brief moment. Surprised, Cheryl had to back up in her assessment of the woman. Perhaps Doll was a persona she wore for the occasion.

"I can work wonders," Cheryl said, "but I'm not a magician and I won't kid you. It may very well take longer than a couple of weeks to accomplish the job. I could move established plants there for a quick fix, but it would be expensive. I don't recommend it."

"Lovey wouldn't want me to be cheap. He wants only the best. You know, like me!" She giggled in a high-pitched voice and gave a tiny wave toward Lovey who smiled back at her.

Cigar smoke hung like a smelly wreath around his head.

"I have some well-planted container gardens," Cheryl said. "Would you like to see them? We could move them over to your place for the party. It would make up for the size of the new plantings."

"We'll be right back, Lovey," Blondie called out, flapping her be-ringed hand over her shoulder and tripping on spike heels behind Cheryl.

"Pssttt."

Cheryl whirled around, scanning the yard. What was that? Did the sound come from the hedge? She must have imagined it.

She saw no one. Blondie was cooing to her pup, holding him over an overflowing container of mixed perennials in full bloom. It was one of the containers she was certain could be transported to her client's property.

"Ppstttttt!"

The sound was accompanied by the rustle of foliage.

Cheryl heard the noise more insistently and finally traced it to the hedge between her yard and that of the detective. She walked over.

"Larkin! What do you want? Can't you see I'm working?" she hissed into the wall of greenery.

"You should stay far away from those people, Cher," he whispered hoarsely. "Not nice." The hedge trembled with his movements, but he stayed well hidden.

"Clients!" she hissed back between clenched teeth. Would he never leave her alone? He was like a tornado that whirled into her life abruptly, tossed her about, and left a wide swath of destruction behind. She steeled her emotions and resolved to never allow him . . .

"Just do as I say, stubborn woman," he whispered firmly. "I'll be over after they leave. Just get rid of them," he demanded, rustling the leaves fiercely.

"I have no intention of doing anything of the sort! Now go away. I'm working." She stalked away from the hedge and stood beside Blondie who was allowing her tiny dog to attempt to lift a leg into a carefully cultivated speedwell border. It fell over and scrabbled around for a bit in the deep turf trying to regain its balance. Over her shoulder, Cheryl could hear the hedge rustling angrily, but her neighbor kept quiet.

"These pots are very nice. How soon can we get them over to my house?" Blondie paused to croon to her dog that was finally recovered and now sniffing at a lush bed of purple, fragrant catmint. It nosed inside the flowers carefully, then finally reached up and clamped his tiny teeth around one stalk.

"Pooky, Pooky. Come away from that. Those plants could be poisonous to you. Come to Mommy, honey." Trembling on palsied legs, the tiny yellow dog made his way gingerly like an old man over to his mistress's side where she quickly scooped him up and stuffed him back into the silk bag. He gave a tiny sigh and seemed to sink into a stupor. An image of the dormouse from *Alice in Wonderland* flashed through Cheryl's mind and she suppressed a giggle.

Probably tired him out, she thought. Most exercise he's had all day. She glanced over her shoulder but the hedge remained quiet. Nevertheless, she guided her client through the thick green turf and back to the front of the shop where Toledo awaited. She invited them both inside and made appointments to conclude their business. Lovey Toledo was generous with a down payment, which Cheryl tucked inside her shirt pocket. She tried on a polite smile and waited for them to leave.

"Nothing but the best for my honey," he said, pinching his girlfriend on the cheek.

Blondie grinned and simpered back at him although Cheryl thought for sure there would be a bruise there later. The lady obviously earned her way.

Cheryl waved them goodbye. She was about to earn her money as well. It would be a definite challenge. Perhaps Honey the Blondie would allow her free rein to do as she thought best. Or perhaps she would look over her shoulder and demand an instant planting of blue cut flowers. Perhaps lisianthus. The Echo species had a very nice blue, which Cheryl thought she could produce from a favorite florist she knew. Otherwise, she would need to figure out a way to plant gladiolas already in bloom. Not impossible, but not desirable and not sure she could produce a true blue either. It was the type of puzzle she enjoyed solving and she was certain she could rise to the challenge.

She wandered back into her shop to write up a plan. This was going to be an extensive job with only two weeks to accomplish a new look. She gave the parrot a few sunflower seeds, and then sat at her desk to sketch.

"I told you to get rid of those people!" Larkin startled her as he burst into the room almost taking her bell off the door. "Have you no sense?" He took her by her shoulders and pulled her up, tipping her chair into a blue ceramic planter filled with a large jade plant. It smashed and scattered soil and buttons of jade leaves across the floor.

"Smack his rear! Awk! Naughty Boy!" the parrot squawked in Nana's voice.

"Get your hands off me, you beast!" Cheryl shook off his hands and kneeled to rescue her plant. "Look what you've done. How many more plants are you going to kill? Turn me loose!" She glanced back at him as he stepped away rubbing his hand against his brow.

"You don't understand, but you need to listen to me, Cher. Those people are not the sort for you to hang around."

Cheryl frowned, glaring over her shoulder at him. "Please leave my shop, Larkin. I think you've done enough harm for one day." She continued to gingerly pick through the broken glass, then rose to find a new planter on a shelf behind her desk.

Larkin drew in a deep breath and tried visibly to calm himself. "You're such a baby, Cher. You always were. Just this one time, will you listen to me? I do know what I'm talking about. You could place yourself in danger if you continue to deal with that man. What did he want, anyway?" He grabbed a trashcan and knelt beside her to pick up glass fragments, dumping them in with unnecessary force. *Clunk! Clunk!*

"The same thing most people want from me. Advice about his gardens. What could possibly be dangerous about that? I think you've finally lost your marbles, Detective."

"That big pile of monstrosity up on the hill? I'd of thought it was covered with gravel." He angrily tossed more broken crockery into the trashcan.

"His blond honey is the one who wants the gardens fixed up. She's giving me two weeks to have it whipped into shape. It's going to tax my powers of invention."

He held out a branch of the jade plant with an apologetic shrug. Cheryl shook her head. The houseplant probably needed transplanting anyway. It was pretty root bound, but she wouldn't let him entirely off the hook. He slipped back on his haunches and gazed directly into her eyes. She knew what was coming. This was his best friend persona that usually managed to talk her into the worse and most dangerous adventures.

"Sweetheart, please take my advice. I can't explain just now, but you need to call those people up and tell them you can't do the work. Pretend you're sick or something." He rested his hand lightly on her shoulder.

Her insides shivered with emotion, but she was determined he wouldn't know what effect he had on her.

"David," she said, "this is my job. It's what I do. I'm not always able to choose my clients on the basis of whether they are nice people or not. Sometimes I don't even like them myself. But they're paying me good money for my services and I intend to earn it."

He stared at her, and she wondered briefly why it was that long, gorgeous eyelashes always seemed to be on the fellows.

There was danger, familiar danger, if she allowed herself to sink into those fascinating eyes, chocolate pools of temptation. She stiffened her resolve, vowing she would not fall into his web this time. She stood up abruptly and walked toward the back room.

He stayed on his knees, staring after her for a moment. Then he released a huge sigh, stood, and walked toward the door muttering. "Not once in all these years has that stubborn little girl listened to anything I had to say to her. Not one darn time!"

"I'm sorry about your shiny, green plant," he called over his shoulder. "I didn't mean to kill it. I hope it gets better."

The door slammed and all was quiet.

Cheryl stood in the back room tucking yet another stem of the jade plant into a new pot. "Wonder what that was all about," she said, addressing the mutilated plant. "Oh well, he's just on another rant. Best to ignore him."

She was pleased her pulse had quieted all on its own without her having to concentrate as she usually did. She might have a handle on this thing between them after all. She moved over to change the water in the parrot's dish and to chat in a soothing, low voice.

Ganymede still paced nervously back and forth on her perch, but refrained from the raucous squawking Cheryl dreaded. Nana had loved her bird, but Cheryl considered its care mostly an obligation. Parrots lived long lives and for all Cheryl knew Gany was in her twilight years needing peace and quiet.

A sigh escaped her as she wandering around the shop. She not only missed her wonderful neighbor lady from next door, she missed her grandmother even more. That good lady had sheltered her from the overbearing woman who mothered her, standing between the pressures of a disappointed parent. Cheryl had fled her home and lived almost solely at her grandmother's. What a fuss her mother had made when Cheryl decided to leave the business world and seek a degree in horticulture and landscaping. Her thoughts drifted back to a pair of chocolate-brown eyes with scandalous long eyelashes.

They made a strange pair, she and her childhood friend. David had once confessed that he had a common background of an ethnic here and an ethnic there all mixed together. Springing from a long line of ancestors, blue-collar parents and grandparents, Larkin was the rollicking counterpart to the quiet young girl next door. She didn't know for sure, but she thought both David's parents worked.

Her grandmother mentioned once that his neighborhood wasn't the best in the world, and her parents worried he was involved with the wrong crowd. He was more closely monitored at his grandmother's and spent most of his time there.

Cheryl's mother considered her family to boast of the bluest of blood but said not a word when her mother moved into this delightful, modest home after her father died to devote herself to gardening. Working in the yard as a hobby was one thing, Cheryl and her grandmother were happiest digging in the dirt and pulling weeds together, but her mother was horrified when Cheryl announced she intended to make a career out of gardening.

"You'll work as a slave, a servant to others, daughter. Why would you want to do that? Your fingernails! How will you . . .? Your father should talk to you. Have you told your father about this? Oh, Cheryl, this is the most bizarre behavior you've ever . . . Why are you so very stubborn?" She had commenced an all-out campaign to change her daughter's mind. So far, she had failed.

When she was young, Cheryl's imagination had her ancestors stepping off the *Mayflower* dressed in the latest fashions and sporting pockets full of silver. Her grandmother laughed and said not quite. She had attempted to explain new as versus old money, but it bored a restive young girl who was often ignored by her parents.

Her father was distracted by his growing business ventures and her mother was newly elected to the Woman's

Club where she happily served on many committees. Grandmother's house was so much more exciting, and then there was the wild boy next door.

That night, dragging herself out of a sound sleep, Cheryl sat up in bed wondering what noise had disturbed her. Someone breaking into the shop? Then she heard it again. Rustling noises coming from her kitchen. Afraid to move, she drew in a shallow breath. Never had she been afraid of living alone in this house even though she was aware the neighborhood had changed over the years. It still felt safe to her. It was Nana's house.

What could anyone want? There was an insignificant amount of cash, but it was in the cash register in the front room. She had nothing worth stealing in her kitchen, for goodness' sake. The memory of Larkin's warning scuttled through her brain, alarming her and sending a surge of adrenalin racing through her veins. *What if he were right about her new clients*? She almost froze in fright.

She swung her feet over the side of the bed just as a shadow loomed in the doorway. From the faint light filtering through her window she could see a dark body moving toward her bed. She got ready to scream for all she was worth. A hand groped her shoulder. Heart pounding, she gave peel after peel of piercing screams as she scooted backward in her bed.

"For God's sake, Cher. Would you cut out that noise? You could damage a fellow's eardrums." Larkin slid to the floor beside her bed and leaned his head on her pillow.

Hyperventilating, Cheryl couldn't speak, but she kicked her feet in frustration and anger. "How dare you scare me like this? Brute!" How many times had he jumped out at her and terrified her over the years, always thinking it was funny. Had he ever staked a claim to Neanderthal ancestry? Perhaps those broad shoulders were from a direct line of cave dwellers. What was the difference between a club and a gun?

"Ouch, will you cut it out? You'd think you were being murdered. I just wanted to chat for a bit. Settle down, honey. Settle." He captured one of her feet and slowly massaged her instep. "There, I didn't mean to scare you. You're okay, right?"

"How did you get into my house?" she finally managed to say. "I want you to leave right now!" In spite of how wonderful her foot felt, she kicked it away from his questing fingers.

"I will in a bit. Talk to me for a while first, will you? I couldn't sleep. Do you think Grandma forgave me for not coming to see her? I feel so bad about it."

"How did you get into my house?" Cheryl repeated, bouncing a bit on the bed. A strange, masculine fragrance tickled her nose. Beer, maybe? Shaving cream? Sweat? Probably a mixture of all three she decided. It was not unpleasant, but was decidedly dangerous to her well-being.

"Answer me, Larkin," she demanded, grabbing a handful of thick black hair and giving it a tug.

"Don't do that, Cher. You have no idea what kind of day I've had. I need a soothing hand up there. Help me out, will you?" He rubbed his head against her leg.

"Okay, but not until you tell me how you got into my house." With her hand poised over his head, she waited.

"I have a key." He reached up and put her hand on his head and rubbed it back and forth.

"A key! How on earth did you get a key?" She pulled his hair gently, and then rubbed her fingers through it soothingly.

He groaned with pleasure and scooted closer to her. "It was just there. I imagine you have one to my house. Our grandmothers were friends, remember? I found it hanging right beside the back door. In the morning, look and see if there's one by yours."

She was using both hands now giving him a slow, steady massage across his head and down his neck. The muscles were corded in his shoulders, and she dug in to convince them to release. He muttered something about her golden fingers and scooted over so he was between her dangling legs with his back turned to her.

"Sweet, sweet, Cher." He wrapped his arms around her legs and leaned back against the bed while she continued to attack his aching muscles.

"Having a key does not give you the right to walk into my house, Beast. I have not given you permission, and my nana's permission is rescinded."

He turned his head and kissed the inside of her thigh. "But I needed you, Sweetheart. You're the only one in the world who could ever make my head stop hurting like this." His head lolled on his shoulders, and she knew her task was almost over. He was relaxing.

"We're not children anymore, David. Grownups don't behave like this." She pulled softly on one of his ears and briefly rested her cheek on top his head. She was tired and close to falling asleep again. "It's time for you to go home and back to bed. I have to work tomorrow and so do you."

A soft snore answered her. *Now what? The big lug is sound asleep on the floor of my bedroom.*

"David?" She shook him but he held tightly to her legs. A giggle escaped into the darkened room as she contemplated her predicament. She wriggled her toes then leaned over and whispered, "David? If you get up, you can sleep in my bed."

He stood and fell into bed beside her, wrapping his arms around her and pulling her tight against him. His breath tickled her hair, and she heard his snore again.

He was sound asleep in her bed. There was nothing for her to do but sleep on the couch. She rested against his warmth for a few minutes enjoying the closeness, inhaling his scent. His size dwarfed her and made her feel ultra-feminine. This man was a bundle of temptation, and she already knew how vulnerable she could be to his charms. Time to go.

She eased out of his arms and padded to the hall closet for a blanket and extra pillow. *Saving this old couch was a good idea. I can feel the presence of my nana tonight. I bet she's laughing at the big lug sleeping in my bed. She always thought you were a good-looking rascal, although she thought you needed more discipline.* Soon Cheryl grinned into the darkness and fell asleep.

She woke to the smell of brewing coffee and sat up rubbing her eyes. Disoriented, she took a minute to remember her visitor from last night. She had fallen into a dreamless sleep and had no idea if the detective had gotten back to his own house or if he was in the kitchen eating her cold cereal. She wrapped the blanket around her shoulders and shuffled to the bathroom. Ugh, she thought, looking at her curls standing up in total disarray. She refreshed herself and headed to the kitchen still wrapped like a mummy in her blanket. It was time she took control of her own home.

As she suspected, Larkin was standing at the sink drinking a cup of steaming coffee. When he turned around, his face was wreathed by a broad smile. She steeled herself to resist it even while her pulse jumped in response. He took one step and enveloped her, blanket and all, in a bear hug.

"Thank you, sweet Cher. I am late to work." He was halfway to the door before she could react. "I'll see you later tonight," he said over his shoulder, and with a bang on the screen door, he was gone.

Cheryl found herself standing in the middle of her kitchen wondering if she had lost her mind. Why hadn't she expressed her anger and told him to stay on his side of the hedge, beast man, killer of lilies and potted plants?

Chapter 4

"Gardening, a Work in Progress"
by Cheryl

Many gardeners plant their flowers to change with the seasons. I have a friend who starts out in the spring with bulbs—hyacinths, grape hyacinths, scilla, and daffodils—of yellows, pinks, and blues. Further along in the spring season, late tulips turn her front bed into a fiery blaze of yellow and red. This is followed by a perennial showing of purple alliums, columbine in blues, and old-fashioned bleeding hearts in arcs of rosy pinks. In July, her gardens are a riot of color that starts with Asiatic lilies, oriental, then trumpet. And so on it goes with a final curtain call of colorful mums. When one show fades, another is in the wings waiting its turn. Bulb planting in the fall generates the excitement of waiting for the blossoms to show color in the spring when weary winter eyes welcome the bright colors.

Cheryl wiped the sweat out of her eyes and considered going inside to an air-conditioned room. The temperature had climbed too far into the 80's for her taste. If she'd wanted to swelter, she'd have moved to Florida, for heaven's sake. She had a good start on her weekly column and tons of work to do inside. *Done. You talked me into it.* She had closed her laptop and twisted her body toward the back door when she heard a car beep its horn. Looking over her shoulder, she spotted a redhead waving gaily at her as she approached with a definite bounce in her step.

"Jane! Hi. I was thinking of calling you this afternoon. You must have ESP. It's good to see you."

"Dunno about that, but I do know I have donuts." She held up a bag already greasy with sin from the bakery.

Her friend Jane was like a torch lily with her slender figure and flaming hair with a jubilant personality to match. It would be difficult to maintain a dour attitude around her. She was a welcome sight any time.

Cheryl wondered what tidbits of gossip and news gleaned from her job at the local town newspaper Jane would share today. Jane thought Cheryl lived an exciting life, but, in truth, it was she who kept in touch with the outside world. Cheryl's good friend Beverly Hampton was the owner and editor of the paper now that her father was semi-retired.

Cheryl winced as she remembered promising Beverly to call for a luncheon date. She'd need to postpone until this job was finished. Two weeks was a very short window for a job that size.

"I thought you'd be working today. Didn't you have a new lucrative job offer?" Jane handed over the donuts.

They settled around the kitchen table, and Cheryl poured them both glasses of frosty iced tea. Without any more delay, they dug into the donut bag with gusto.

"I do. A man named Sam Toledo and his significant other hired me to transform their gardens for a big blowout party. I have some soil being delivered today and other maintenance work on-going. I was there for three hours early this morning, but I can't do anything more until they finish. What are you up to today?"

"Oh, this and that. I'm having an errand day, but thought I'd take a break and catch up on gossip with you."

"I was thinking you might like to go on an adventure." Cheryl glanced at her obliquely. "I'm on a rescue mission this evening right before dark." She laughed when Jane clapped her hands and welcomed the news with an eager smile.

"Well. What is it? Do I need to dress a certain way? Do I need a bucket this time? Last time you boosted me over a wall and we snitched armfuls of lilacs from that old meatpacking plant. God knows who planted them there in the first place, but we didn't have a thing to hold water." She laughed at the memory. "Security guard almost caught us too."

"Old fuddy-duddy." Cheryl shook her half-eaten donut in the air. "Like anyone cared about those lilacs. He was just bored and needed something to do. That place has been closed for years." She munched down on a grape jelly donut, loving how it squished down her fingers. Good thing she got lots of exercise.

"You need to be careful, Jane. I'm safe because the calories are half as potent if you haven't paid for them, but you, dear lady, are in trouble." She laughed again at the shocked expression on her friend's face.

"No really, Cheryl. It's not true, is it?" She looked down at her slender form with horror.

"Jane, you could gain ten pounds, and I'd never find where you'd put it. Just teasing you."

"My mother said as I get closer to thirty my backside would start to spread into a huge thing." She returned the sticky donut to the bag with a sad face.

Cheryl knew Jane's mother did indeed own an enormous rear end, but she doubted it could ever happen to Jane, who more readily resembled her rail-thin father.

They both jumped when they heard three loud knocks on the back door before it swung open abruptly and banged against the wall. David Larkin, hair too long and still wet from his shower, marched in, plopped down in a chair, and grabbed the bag. With his mouth already devouring half a donut, he turned to Jane and tweaked her red curls.

"Hey," he mumbled, mingling the greeting with his donut.

Cheryl snorted as Jane's face turned bright red. Larkin was up to his old tricks again.

"What's exciting at the paper, Jane? Anyone get shot, robbed, or otherwise abused?" He reached for his second pastry.

"Pretty quiet today, David. You know about that dog that got hit? Vet fixed him up, but they still don't know who the owner is. The fire down at the bowling alley was just a grease fire. Was all out before the fire trucks got there. Some excitement over a man who paid cash for a piece of property. Not sure which one. I was on a break when they were discussing it."

"Yeah? Did he bring the money in a paper bag? Old rusty tin can dug up from the backyard? Must not have been much of a property. Who's got that kind of dough these days?" David chuckled with Jane who had not a clue what he was referring to, but was amiable. She was bombarded with snatches of news from her job, but rarely understood the importance or lack of the information.

"Did you hear about the number of tickets the police were giving out after the game the other night?" Jane asked, forgetting that David Larkin was a cop. Instead of answering, he whirled around, catching Cheryl by surprise.

"Did you get rid of Toledo?" he asked, impaling her with fierce eagle eyes that had the golden flecks flashing. "You have no business dealing with the criminal element. You're just a baby yourself," Larkin chewed his words out through an enthusiastic mouthful of donut. He reached over and then trailed a finger down her cheek probably leaving a sticky steak of jam on her face.

Cheryl could hear Jane take a gulp and saw her shift in her seat. No doubt about it, her friend had a soft spot for the detective.

"If they're criminals, why don't you arrest them?" Cheryl challenged. She absolutely refused to allow David Larkin to think he could run her life. And, whatever reactions she had to his masculinity, she would keep to herself. Half the county no doubt had sampled that careless charm. Darned if she would get in line for anyone. He would learn she was an adult and wasn't going to play his fool while he adventured. Would he ever stop treating her as if she were still a child? She'd gotten rid of Gordon for just that very thing. She glared at David but declined to engage him in an argument.

"Cher, honey, sweet thing . . . you're cute as a button, but I need to make you understand. There are just some people you should stay away from. Sam Toledo has a police record which would amaze you. He may come off as civilized, but believe me, he isn't. I don't know that chick he's hanging with, but, for sure, she's up to no good if she finds his company welcome. I'll find out who she is today."

"I don't always get to choose my clients, Larkin," Cheryl snapped. "In case you haven't noticed, I run a business, not a social register." She glanced over at Jane but could see there would be no help from her.

Her friend was staring at the detective, her eyes already glazing over. David was no help. As she watched, he grinned at Jane who flashed as red as her tablecloth, but still managed to smile back.

She hastily turned her face in apology and shrugged her shoulders helplessly. Cheryl struggled to contain her amusement at her transparent friend. From the time they were in kindergarten, what you saw was what you got with her best friend. Talk about stable character. Jane's was formed in stone. Cheryl found comfort in the knowledge that some things never change and pleased that there was no need.

"Clients!" Larkin exploded. "Those are not clients. They are criminals! Didn't you hear what I said, you little goose?" He hit his fist on the table and then stood up, sliding his chair nosily across the floor.

"I don't have a clue what those two are up to," David said, "but, if it's about gardening, I'll wear ballet shoes to work. Just do what I told you for a change, Cher. Just do." He straightened the part of his shirt covering the butt of his revolver, nodded to Jane, and banged the door again on his way out.

"Awk! Don't slam the door. Don't slam the door, you naughty boy." Polly screamed, sounding so much like Cheryl's grandmother they burst into laughter.

"He's a bit peeved with you, Cheryl," Jane said pensively. "What's it all about?"

"Nothing important. David, Detective Larkin, thinks he has a right to dictate my life to me just because he's moved into his grandmother's house next door. Notice how successful he is." She deliberately turned her back to the window.

"He's one handsome hunk. I don't know how you can stand having him living right so close to you. I think my insides would be in jelly all day, never mind the nights. Have you peeked through the hedge?" She drew the curtain back on the kitchen window and peered across the yard.

"No, and I don't intend to. He and his buddies are noisy enough. They're destroying that beautiful garden his grandmother worked on for so many years. Volleyball, would you believe?" Cheryl stuffed the last of the donut into her mouth and sipped her tea.

"Policemen have to stay in shape," Jane said, nodding wisely like the schoolteacher she wasn't.

"They have gyms for that sort of thing. Enough about my pushy neighbor. We need to make plans for our excursion tonight."

Never hesitating to enter into Cheryl's plans, Jane listened eagerly to her best friend.

Brambles, weedy shrubs, and dense undergrowth grew thickly around the rusty iron fence, a tribute to an earlier gracious period of time. Its ornate design captured Cheryl's attention momentarily as she speculated on a possible entry into the property. So sad to see it rusting away, and they could not budge it open.

Jane stared at the huge stands of briars dubiously. "Are you sure?" she whispered. "I can't believe anything's left of the gardens. I remember them when I was in grade school. My mother took me on a tour with some church ladies. Very formal. Always made me want to whisper even outdoors."

Cheryl shook a loose corner of the hedge and gained an advantage. "I guess there's no one left who wants the old place. Some distant relatives have sold it, I think, to a developer. In a few weeks, we'll no doubt see a complex of apartments and townhouses here. A bulldozer will destroy any plants left. I wanted to rescue as many of the peonies as I could." She managed to squeeze through the broken bar and reached back to pull her shovel through. "Throw me that bushel basket before you come in, will ya?"

"Ouch! Not on my head." Cheryl heard Jane giggle but couldn't see her through the brush. "Come on in. I don't think anyone cares if we're here."

"Snakes might. This place just reeks of snakes. And probably rats. Big hairy rats with red eyes that bite you on the ankle." Jane stepped gingerly through the weeds trying to stay as close to Cheryl as she could. Her spade dragged behind her.

"Pick up your shovel. You'll attract company with all that noise." Cheryl stood up on an ancient, rotting stump to survey the entire yard. Massive overgrown yews meandered wildly, some dead, most beyond recognition as the original gardens sentries. She spotted a wide path almost obscured by grasses and guessed where it would lead. Dusk was not far away. They needed to hurry.

"I have my bearings now," Cheryl said firmly. She spotted thorny brambles up the path and tucked her arms to her side. "The peony bed is over in that corner adjacent to the side porch of the house. Just step high and don't bump into that tickseed or you'll be wearing most of it. The seeds stick to everything."

Too late. Jane had them stuck to her jeans and embedded in her hair, brown accents in the red curls. Cheryl stifled a smile. Her friend was not a plant person and rarely recognized even a dandelion. They'd need to de-seed her later. She didn't want those seeds spread into her own weed-free gardens.

They picked their way carefully and slowly through fallen limbs, leaves, and other debris that had collected over the years. A pungent smell of deep woods filled the air with the accumulated bits and pieces of summers past. The last occupant in the gracious old house had been an elderly lady too infirmed to garden and too poor to hire the work done.

Huge trees, centuries old, shaded them as they wound their way through the overgrowth of weeds and scrap saplings. The setting sun peeked through the branches, flickering in and out. Cheryl would love to rejuvenate this beautiful old garden. Too late now. The property was sold.

"I always wanted to see the inside of this house," Jane whispered from behind her. "Let's go peek in the window." She jumped and grabbed Cheryl when they heard a rustle behind them. "What's that?" she squeaked frantically. "Snakes?"

"More likely a little chickadee or a towhee." Cheryl peered in the direction of the noise.

"Oh, my God! Do they bite?" Jane squeezed Cheryl's arm painfully as she hid her face.

"Birds, silly. They are birds that scratch in the leaves hunting for worms and such." Cheryl grabbed Jane's hand and pulled her forward.

"Worms? What kind of worms? Do they bite? Are they slimy?" Jane huddled closer as they walked together toward the house. The windows, beautifully rounded and carved, were higher than they expected. They stood eyeing them pensively for a moment. The silence was broken in an occasional swirl of the dry leaves by puffs of an indolent breeze.

"There's a concrete block over there. Help me slide it over closer to the house." Cheryl waded through the almost-shoulder-high weeds carefully avoiding the tickseed cling-ons and motioned to Jane to help her tug the heavy block.

"Perfect." Jane jumped up on the block and peered through the window. "Ewee. Dirty. Nice room though. Wow, wait until you see. The chandelier is still there complete with all the crystals. Must be hundreds of them. They need a good cleaning but still lovely. Here, take a look." She stepped down and moved over to allow Cheryl to take a peek.

Cheryl stepped on the block and was squinting through the dirty window when a movement caught her eye and she took a quick breath. Something . . . someone was inside the house. She braced her hands on the wall in front of her and moved closer to peer inside. *What was going on?* She reached down and grabbed Jane by the shoulder, her finger against her lips shushing her.

"There's a man inside with a gun!"

Jane's gasp had Cheryl scrambling down and slamming her hand over her friend's mouth.

"Quiet!" Cheryl said. "Let me see what's going on and then we'd better get out of here." She stepped back on the concrete block and strained to see inside the darkened room. Nothing. Whoever was inside had passed through the room and left.

Just as Cheryl was about to step down, a man entered the dining room again holding a gun pointed at a second man. She could hear the menacing tone as one threatened the other. The voice was faint but she recognized it. She knew the man. Sam Toledo. David was right! This was no place for the two of them to be. She froze when she heard the sound of a gunshot. Dear God! From her vantage point, neither of them was visible. *Did Sam kill someone?*

Her involuntary scream was stifled as someone grabbed her from behind and covered her mouth firmly with his hand. Terror seized her, and her blood froze. She resisted, pulling fiercely against the force holding her. She sidestepped off the concrete block and almost fell to her knees. A strong arm encircled her waist and steadied her upright.

"Shhhh. Be quiet, Cher. I've got you. Come quickly." The familiar fragrance of Larkin's shaving lotion penetrated her consciousness. She recognized him before she turned around to see David and another policeman who had an arm around Jane and was hurrying her back through the garden. David was holding her around the waist snugly and way too familiarly. He rubbed his face against hers as they walked rapidly away. She glared at him only to be faced with a wide grin.

"Now, Cher, we got to get you out of here, honey. This is no place for two young ladies to be."

Never mind that she agreed with him, Cheryl deeply resented being told what to do by the same pushy neighbor. *Where in the world had he come from?*

"What's going on, David? I saw a man with . . . it was a gun!"

He leaned over and gently kissed her on the mouth, causing her to gasp as the sensation bolted throughout her system.

"So tasty, little Cher. You always were so tasty." He tugged her behind an ancient yew tree and dipped his head.

She grabbed on to his shoulders to brace herself, her thoughts scattering for a minute before she could regain her composure.

"Wait a minute. Stop that! You can't just decide to kiss me any time you please. Who do you think you are, David Larkin? I know you're trying to distract me." It took all her will to look him in the eye while her body betrayed her longing and nudged her otherwise. Never had her hormones been so close to rebellion. Okay, once before when he kissed her, but that didn't count. She'd been a child and didn't know better.

"No? But it's so much fun." He gave her a tender swipe, nibbling her lips and trailing kisses across her cheek, and then turned reluctantly away. "I'll make a deal with you if you'll go quietly with me out of here." He turned them toward the back gate as night fell and the shadows deepened around them.

In the distance, a streetlight shone weakly. She could just see the white grin on David's face as he peered down at her. Cheryl looked behind her at the hulking figures created by the wild yews and other neglected shrubs. She shuddered, wondering what evil was roaming in this overgrown garden abandoned for so many years.

"I'll let you know exactly what's going on after we get back to your house," David said. "Deal?"

Reluctantly she nodded, forgetting about her spade and basket. He took her by the hand and, smiling down at her tenderly, wound their way back through the weedy path, only once trailing his hand—now in the guise of a Frenchman or was he still in Italian Stallion mode?—too low on her back. By the time they returned exhausted and tired, Jane and she agreed to forgo the meeting until the following day.

"You promised! You know you did."

It was early the next morning and Jane sat watching the two of them.

"Hey, you two, I feel like a spectator in a tennis match," Jane said as Cheryl raged at her old nemeses.

David had unwisely chosen to play the "I'm an undercover cop" card and was keeping mum about the men Cheryl had spotted in the old Hansen mansion.

"Look. No one was shot. One of those men was threatening the other, but he didn't shoot him. Actually I think they're partners, but we aren't sure of that just yet." Larkin stood at the kitchen sink making baloney sandwiches from a package of meat he had brought over from his refrigerator.

Cheryl suppressed a shudder as she watched him. As if she would ever buy such disgusting food as that. Without speaking, she watched him slice into one of her beautiful homegrown tomatoes and slap mayo liberally across a slice of wheat bread. He added a lettuce leaf before topping it with the slice of bread and plunking it down on a paper napkin in front of her.

"Jane?" He raised his thick, black eyebrows at her friend who nodded enthusiastically.

"I saw Sam Toledo, David, with my own eyes. You said he was a criminal and now I believe you. He was holding a gun pointed directly at the other man, and then I heard a gunshot. How can you say nothing happened?"

"I just can. Leave it at that, will you? You are the most annoying, nosy, little sweet thing I ever met. Eat your sandwich, honey. Everything is under control. What were the two of you doing out there in the first place? On an owl prowl?"

"Oh, no! My shovel. And my basket." Cheryl locked eyes with Jane who shook her head vigorously.

"Not now, not never! I'm not going back into that jungle for anything. You can just forget it, Cheryl." Jane picked up her sandwich and bit firmly into it.

Larkin grinned as he sat down at the table with his.

"I see you found some seeds to share." He tugged an embedded seed from the back of her hair.

"Tick seeds in my hair too? Ack!" Cheryl twisted around as if she could see the back of her head and felt for the irritating seeds tangling her unruly mop.

Jane pushed her hand into her matted red head and tugged on an embedded seed. "I have a few I picked up myself." She yanked and then squealed loudly when the tickseed resisted. Cheryl beckoned and then, stepping to Jane's back, began to deseed her friend. It was a tedious job, but finally she located every one. She patted her friend on the shoulder and regained her seat at the table.

"Antique peonies. We were trying to rescue a plant or two of those gorgeous old peonies over in the corner adjacent to the house. I heard the bulldozers were on their way. We forgot our basket and spades," she said regretfully around a very satisfying mouthful of baloney sandwich. She didn't want to waste the bread since it was already made into a sandwich.

"Are you saying that Sam Toledo bought the property?" She watched Larkin's face change from her congenial neighbor to the cop persona again.

"Cheryl, sweets, I am not saying anything. The subject is closed. You and Jane stay away from that place. You have your clients to take care of, remember?"

"No way! I'm calling Toledo tomorrow and canceling the job. He might shoot me if he thinks I haven't done a good enough job." She poured hot coffee for the three of them.

"Err, about that. Let's not be so hasty. You're being paid a lot of money to do that design job. And you're hoping that it will build your business. Perhaps you should keep it for now." He blandly munched a large bite of his sandwich.

Cheryl turned around and stared at him with her mouth hanging wide open. She closed it and sat down, sticking her face right next to his.

"Why, now that I agree with you about the criminal aspects of Sam Toledo, are you encouraging me to continue to work for him?" A kernel of suspicion crept through her brain only to be forced back. Surely not.

"Shot! She might get shot!" Jane said in a half panic. "You don't want Cher to get shot, do you?" She reached over and grabbed on to Cheryl's arm and squeezed it hard.

"It's okay, Jane. I have no intention of continuing the association, no matter what brain freeze David has gotten himself into this time. Probably all that volleyball he plays. When you are as old as he is, it's dangerous to your health."

"Do me a favor, hon. Just sleep on it." He stood up, patting her hair, before sliding his hand down the side of her face. He cupped her chin forcing her to look up at him. Cheryl tried to still her pulse. The beast was on the loose again. No telling where he might land. She would resist as usual.

"Jane, I'm asking you to keep this episode quiet for now, will you? As a personal favor just for me?" He impaled Jane with his chocolate-brown eyes, and Cheryl watched her visibly melt.

"I won't tell anyone, David, I promise," Jane said, her hands clasped beneath her chin as if in prayer.

Cheryl snorted.

The floor of the cottage vibrated as the Neanderthal detective crossed the kitchen and left by the back door, his absence creating a vacuum of sound and movement. Jane finally stirred, whispering wistfully that she thought she'd better head for home.

Cheryl just nodded, sitting quietly for a moment before rising and seeing her to the door.

"Weird adventure this time. I'm sorry, Jane. I'll call you tomorrow."

Cheryl heard the rattle of the back door and roused herself from a deep sleep. Had she thought to put the inside latch on? More rattling, then silence. She lay awake, a sliver of a moon causing almost no threat to the darkness. What were her feelings for David Larkin, playboy cop of the county? She was certainly aware of what her girly hormones thought, but who could trust those? He was a big bruiser of a man, ruggedly handsome with a smile that could strip the bark off living trees. He'd been in and out of her life from childhood, careless of her feelings, but irresistible all the same. She'd always been drawn to him like a magnet clipped to the refrigerator. Thank goodness they hadn't connected all that often. He alternately treated her like a big brother with an annoying little sister or a casual would-be lover who was attracted to her when he paused long enough to really take notice.

She twisted in the sheets. It was hard to practice deception when she was alone with her private thoughts. In all honesty, she had a thing for Big David. Had had since she endured puberty at age twelve going on thirteen. Her grandmother had consoled her once when her friend had made a promise and then forgot about it.

"He'll take a bit of growing up before he's worth anything to a good woman," she said to a sobbing, disappointed Cheryl.

Wonder just how much more growing up he needs yet? She turned over, thumped her pillow, and was just drifting off to sleep when she heard a *tap-tap* on her window.

"I don't believe this," she said, getting up and finding her robe. She drew the curtains aside and raised the window just an inch.

"Cher, honey. Let me in. Just for a minute, okay? I really need to talk to you."

"Call me on the phone, David. I'm sleeping. Call me in the morning."

"I won't keep you long. Honest. Let me in, please?" His voice had dropped an octave and had reached the sultry, sexy range. The Italian was here again. She struggled against the sound, determined to resist the pull of his call.

"What do you want that can't wait until morning?" she asked, knowing she was failing.

"Just a point or two that needs clearing up. I need to be gone very early in the morning. Can we chat just for a minute?"

"David." Her exasperation was more for herself than for him. He was just the same as he always was, his selfish needs preceding hers as usual. Situation normal, nothing changed.

"Please, Cher, sweetheart?"

She wondered who else in the neighborhood he was waking.

"All right. Just for a minute. Do you promise?"

"I do, I swear!"

She could hear rustle in the shrubbery at the side of her house. For a moment she wondered if he had been about to climb in through the window. *David, David. You are probably the reason I can't make a match with more eligible men.* She belted her robe and stepped in bare feet toward the back door where indeed she had found on a hook an ancient key to his house. Their grandmothers, living next door to each other, had been best friends as well as neighbors.

As she slide the latch back, the door popped open and she was enfolded by the warm, firm arms of David Larkin, cop by profession, plant killer by day, and seducer of random women by night. He snuggled his head on her neck pulling her tight against his body.

"What is it about you that I need in the night, sweet Cher?" He trailed kisses down her neck and headed south toward her breasts.

"Whoa, big fellow. That's enough of that." She pushed him backward, noting to herself that it was quite clear what it was that he needed in the night, and she thought it prudent to put as much space between his need and her as she could manage. Certainly she could agree that it was a big need indeed. Her own needs she squelched as quickly as she could manage.

"So?" She re-belted her robe wondering how he managed to undress her so adroitly. She hadn't felt a thing.

"Can't I come in?" he asked plaintively.

She could just make out the lines of his face in the almost complete darkness. Trees rustled in a slight breeze and stars twinkled overhead. The night was enchanted and she was in danger of being seduced by a sorcerer. She pushed against his massive chest gently then found his hand and tugged.

"Let's go into the garden, shall we?"

He grunted in agreeable satisfaction and tried to steer her toward the hammock strung between two trees.

"No, no. Let's sit over here on the bench by the goldfish pond. I always wanted to try it out in the night."

He ambled beside her and settled at her side on the stone bench. It was cool to her bottom and a bit scratchy to her bare legs. She realized David, bare footed, wore a pair of tennis shorts and a T-shirt.

"Well?" She held tightly to his hand which was attempting to wander over her person.

"Well, what?" he asked, persisting in the exploration of her robe.

"You said," she said patiently and ponderously, ". . . that you wanted a minute to discuss something with me. What is it?"

"Oh yeah, that. Well, I want to ask a favor of you. When you go to work at Toledo's tomorrow, I need you to keep your eye out for a certain person. Well, two, in fact. I have the pictures at the house. You want to come over and see them now?" He breathed softly on her neck and kissed her there.

She held her breath while he found her ear and kissed it pausing to suck on her earlobe. "David Gillard Larkin. Will you stop it? You could very well show me the pictures in the morning. You said it was important I see them tonight."

"It *was* important that I see you tonight. I needed to see you tonight. Not sure quite why, but am sure I needed . . . You are the only person alive who knows my middle name, Cher. How did you find out? You're going to have to marry me now. Only way to keep the secret." He managed to free his hand and held her face while he whispered a kiss across her lips. He sighed and plunged enthusiastically into her mouth.

The magic night wrapped around Cheryl like soft black velvet. Nothing she could do but hold on for dear life. She felt as if she floated around the garden, her will sapped by the feel of his lips on hers. He pulled her close, and then lifted her easily into his lap, his neediness clearly prominent. Her robe betrayed her as it rode up her legs, leaving her stripped to her bikini underwear. He shifted her until she straddled him, taking her protests into his mouth as he ruthlessly continued to kiss her. He paused briefly and removed his T-shirt over his head, his naked chest warm against her bare . . . *bare? Oh my God.* He had her robe open, her pajama top unbuttoned, and they were naked chest to naked chest.

Cheryl had a brief moment of lucidity. She was no novice. If she allowed this to continue, she knew what would happen, with no one to blame but herself. She knew what kind of man she was making out with in the garden. Handsome rogue, but rogue he was. He would take what he wanted and leave her crying once again. Could she resist the erogenous high he had produced? Her breasts were riding against the nest of his chest hair, titillating the nipples with just enough pressure to drive her wild. Okay, just a minute more and then she'd. . . .

He picked her up and walked rapidly toward the back door all the while continuing to kiss her lips, her face, and trying to kiss her breasts.

"Cher, we need to go inside, honey," he said in a hoarse whisper.

"Absolutely not! Put me down, David. Right now! This is not going to happen tonight. Not tonight, not never. I refuse to be your next-door-in-need girl."

David dropped his arms in surprise, backed up, and tripped over the little garden statue of Pan tucked into a fragrant bed of lavender, his half-goat self piping in a concrete frozen act of seduction.

Perfect. Pan the half man/half goat will find you good company, David Larkin, she thought as she hurried toward the back door.

"What the hell!"

She could hear him floundering in her garden and in the

blackness of the night heard splashing in the lily-covered goldfish pond.

Feeling heady release and freedom from temptation, she ducked inside and slammed the door, locking the night chain against him, and then slid to the floor, a bundle of unfilled urges pounding in her brain. Panting, she ran to her bedroom, jumped in bed, and pulled the covers over her head.

The thought came to her that she need not fear strangers intruding into her home but a familiar figure alternately beloved and disliked from next door. She had come very close to engaging in something that would upset her very much the next day. Hopefully he had not been injured from his encounter with a concrete replica of himself and maybe had even cooled off by a dip with her goldfish.

Chapter 5

"Are you sure this is a good idea?" Cheryl asked. "Yesterday Detective Larkin assured me the best thing to do was to stay away from Sam Toledo. Now he won't tell me why he changed his mind."

An early morning phone call had summoned a bewildered Cheryl. She finally had agreed to an appointment with Chief of Police McCall and Detective Kevin Fowler and had been picked up and given a ride in a black-and-white police car. There had been no sign of her late-night visitor, not even a rustle from the separating hedge.

"And I'm sorry about that, Miss Esterbrook. It's a matter of security. We're in the middle of an investigation and, truly, the less information you have, the safer it will be for you." The middle-aged man smiled at her kindly and reassuringly.

Cheryl was still mystified and filled with residual anger at Larkin for keeping her in the dark, but his boss was going a long way to reconciling her. Why hadn't David explained it to her in a reasonable manner like this man? No, he had to give her an order. Just like him to treat her like a child.

"If we could, we would not involve you in this case, but your position as a worker on the estate has us asking you to help us out, if you can." Detective Fowler pushed a button on his phone and requested fresh coffee.

"Am I safe? David said this man was a criminal and I saw him holding a gun on another man with my own eyes. This doesn't make me anxious to hurry over there and complete the job I was hired to do."

"Yes, it was unfortunate that you stumbled into that meet. We think those two are actually partners in some pretty nefarious activities. Why the gun was out is a mystery even to us. It's difficult for honest men to guess what's in the minds of the criminal, but no one was harmed, I promise you." Chief McCall clasped his hands together as if he believed she would be satisfied with this explanation, then nodded and smiled at her.

"Are they using the old Hansen Mansion for something illegal?" she asked. What did the rumor of the bulldozers mean? Were they contemplating opening up a gambling casino or something equally as threatening to the neighborhood. Surely not. Her imagination was churning overtime, which was exactly what happened when secrets were kept. Why didn't they trust her to understand?

Kevin Fowler reached down and shuffled a folder to the top of a pile of paperwork.

"Does Toledo own . . . has he bought that old place?" she asked.

The chief didn't answer her right away and gazed out the window. After a few minutes, he turned his head and spoke with a nostalgic tone to his voice.

"Our town has been expanding with rapid growth in the last couple of years. Time was when I was mostly acquainted with every citizen. Lately we have been forced to hire new personnel just to keep up with the expansions out on the highway. Sad but true. Small towns do grow, but not always happily." He sighed, then sat up and put his elbows folded on his desk and assumed a very serious expression.

She thought she understood why her friend was attracted to Detective Fowler. He projected the personality of a take-charge kind of person, but with a calmness that inspired trust.

Detective Fowler leaned forward. "Let's talk about your contract with Sam Toledo, shall we? You start work for him again this morning, right?"

"Yes, I've already started the job. I use subcontractors and they've been roughing in some of the designs I've had approved by the clients. I have a landscaper lined up for the larger shrubs and hardscapes. What was it you wanted me to do?" She felt strange and dubious about all these secret doings. Why did they insist on keeping her in the dark? She wasn't the criminal.

"By the way, where is Detective Larkin this morning? I thought he was to meet me at my shop." She sipped her coffee, wondering how soon she could escape. If she was to continue work at the Toledo property, she needed to hurry. Those contractors would charge whether they were actively working or not. Her thoughts drifted to the placements of decorative stones and hidden gardens.

"I'm sure he'll be able to meet with you later today." The chief pushed a button on his phone again and spoke into an intercom. "Anne, will you bring me that Toledo folder?"

Cheryl glanced at Detective Fowler who smiled at her reassuringly once more, while the chief continued to direct.

"We'd like you to be a sort of watch dog for us, if you don't mind. It would really be helpful if you could identify two men for us. Thank you, Anne." He accepted the folder then opened it on his desk. The attractive uniformed woman winked at Cheryl and left the room.

Was she a friend of David's? Probably lover, if she knew David. She deliberately suppressed thoughts along that line. What good did it do anyway?

"Here is person number one. He has several aliases but presently goes by the name of Geer Monger. If he shows up at the Toledo residence, we need to know immediately. We'll give you a cell phone. You don't engage this man in any way. Just identify him and call us. Okay?" He handed Cheryl a photo of a swarthy man with a moustache and a big hooked nose. One ear was pierced by a tiny hoop through the lobe.

Cheryl studied the photo for a minute. "May I have a copy of this?"

"Certainly. This folder is for you. Spend some time studying it until you feel confident you'll recognize this man if you see him. Here is the second person we would like for you to look out for." He passed her a second photo of a gray-haired man whose face seemed younger than his hair. He had a snub nose and thin lips.

"This man also has been known by several different names but at present goes by Tim Griever. He might speak with a slight accent. Again, please do not engage either of these men in conversation. Just notify us they have been spotted . . . discretely if you can." The chief leaned back and nodded to Detective Fowler.

Cheryl wondered what that signal meant but soon figured it out.

Fowler leaned almost imperceptibly forward and spoke slowly but emphatically. "This is important. We do not want you to attract the attention of either Sam Toledo or his friends. You mostly deal with the woman, right?"

"So far. Mr. Toledo is around, but he talks to his wife or girlfriend, not sure which, and she talks to me. How long do you want me to be a lookout? Mrs. Toledo said they were giving a big party in two weeks, and she wanted me finished before then. Not that I can finish in such short time, but I intend to have her place in good enough shape by then, so she can feel confident her party will be a success."

"A party in two weeks?" An arrested glint came into the detective's eyes. "Did she say anything else? How many people were invited, what the occasion was, anything at all?" He spoke rapidly and eagerly.

Cheryl shook her head. "Nothing except that it was to entertain business acquaintances and that it was important for the property to look good. Money was no expense."

"That may be a significant piece of information. You've already been helpful, Ms. Esterbrook, and we certainly appreciate it. I'll see you out."

"Thank you, Detective Fowler, Chief." She picked up the folder, preparing to leave.

"The cell phone is in the folder. Do not to hesitate to call me if you have further questions. I imagine Detective Larkin will be in touch with you soon. Good-bye now."

Maybe I'll be in touch with him. Why me? Darn that man. Always in my face, interfering in my life. Now here I am about to be murdered in my bed—or at least at work. Who are all these people, and how am I to get my work done without worrying about who's packing and who's not.

She skipped down the stairs and onto the street holding the folder close to her chest. As she headed for her car, she bumped into a buxom blonde who was hurrying by.

"Mrs. Toledo! How are you?" Cheryl asked in surprise as she struggled not to drop the folder. Her purse slipped out of her hand and scattered lipstick, keys, a notepad, and a million other items she had considered necessary to carry with her all day. Her pulse raced as she scrambled to gather up the items. The blonde kneeled to help her.

"You probably guessed that I'm not really Mrs. Just call me Francine. Cheryl, isn't it? I'm not married to him but I have a certain role in my honey's life, and I'm really glad to do it." She giggled.

"What are you doing downtown?" Francine continued. "I thought you were going to be working back at the house this morning. Do you need a ride? I'm going back there right now. I had to get my hair done and Ramón was only available this early." She touched her hair, which was a bright blond.

Today she wore a diamond bracelet that slid heavily toward her elbow. Her flamboyant clothing seemed to have been created for a person a couple of sizes smaller. Cheryl wondered how she managed to zip her slacks, they were so tight. *Could she breathe?*

"No, I had an appointment, but I'm on my way there right now. Shall I see you later?" Cheryl asked.

Francine stood looking at her while patting her hair with raised eyebrows, no doubt recently plucked and groomed. Bright sunlight accented the heavy makeup on her face. She nodded and moved as if to find her car.

Cheryl looked up and spotted David Larkin watching her from the doorway of a hardware shop. He shook his head slightly from side to side, indicating she was not to recognize him.

Fine with me if I never recognize you again! What have you gotten me into now? This may be the worst caper since we built that tree house in your grandmother's prize apple tree.

Chapter 6

Detective David Larkin pulled his nondescript cop car slowly to a stop behind a thin stand of roadside brush. He reached for his already cooling take-out coffee and sipped while he stared at the house on the adjacent hill. Mansion would be a better description. Ugly modern-day McMansion all one-story and sprawling in every direction. He could see a fenced-in area, probably the pool with an adjacent building—cabana?—attached. The foundation plantings were formal and stiff. Very little of it. No trees to speak of. It would be impossible to get close enough to survey the activity around it. The grounds were too extensive, broad, at least a couple of acres with almost no cover. He reached for his binoculars and steadied his arm on the open window.

Lots of activity. Most of it generated by a trim little brunette wearing a hard hat and a pair of painter's jeans. Incongruously, bright yellow boots, worn almost to her knees, were like a flashing stoplight to his searching eyes. She carried a clipboard in her hand and was waving to a front-end loader, which seemed about to run her down. It was hauling a . . . what? Rock? Huge boulder. Larkin shook his head. That little girl could get herself into some kinds of messes. He'd always had to look out for her growing up. Her and her big blue eyes, staring up at him so trustingly. He chuckled with a memory of her passing scrap lumber up to him when he was in his Grandma's apple tree. There she stood, silently staring, until he had to pull her up beside him.

Pesky little girl. He had to admit she hadn't flinched when the grandmothers' had punished them both.

Plunked on the back steps for what seemed like hours while she sat beside him forbidden even to talk to each other. Not a single tear. He'd have to give her that. She had guts. Or whatever rich little girls had. Courage probably better named. Just as solemnly, she had stood underneath the apple tree while he ripped his tree house apart and passed the lumber back down to her. Grandma had been upset.

The front-end loader successfully rolled the huge boulder into a crevice already prepared for it in the side of the hill. He watched Cheryl clap her hands enthusiastically and wave happily to the driver who saluted and drove his equipment away. Cheryl walked over to the rock and patted it fondly as if it were a big dog. *God. Did she just hug that stone?*

He could get jealous of that rock. Last night was still swirling around in his head. When did he get so entangled in one woman? He absolutely refused to think about it. He had successfully tabled unsuitable thoughts of Cheryl years ago and couldn't quite figure out why she was back haunting his nighttime dreams.

Here comes the girlfriend. He adjusted the binoculars once more as the brassy blonde came tripping down the hill toward Cheryl. *What a bimbo! And what a contrast she was to the classy lady in the hard hat beside her.* Even in her work clothes, Cheryl stood out as a tribute to her gender. He winced when the blonde put her arm around Cheryl's shoulders. *Wonder where Toledo picked that one up.* He hated that they had had to use Cheryl. It would suit him better if she were miles away and had never heard of Sam Toledo. If only there was another way.

What now?

The front-end loader was rolling toward the two women carrying a good-sized evergreen tree of some sort. Now he saw a hole already dug and prepared for it. Two burly men swarmed down the hill behind the loader and guided the large tree in place. With shovels they back-filled the tree halfway with soil. A truck pulled close and treated the tree with water and what he presumed was fertilizer. The water had a bluish cast.

Two more men rode close in a green and yellow Gator, that sexy little John Deere tractor/truck, and distributed several shrubs. The scene was beginning to make sense. *Who would have believed the little girl knows what she is doing?* He settled down to watch Cheryl turn the Toledo stronghold into something with a bit of class.

She has enough of that. Class, that is. She was born with a silver spoon between her perfect teeth and sexy lips with doting parents fulfilling her every wish. Why she chose to make a living— No, he was certain she didn't need to earn her room and board. Why she enjoyed getting her hands dirty was beyond his comprehension. He noticed her turn toward where he was parked and shade her eyes.

Don't do that, Sweetheart. He squirmed in the seat and put the cold coffee cup in its holder ready to roll if anyone else noticed him lurking there. *Look away, Cher. Look away!*

The blonde said something to her and the two of them walked toward the house and out of sight. David felt his stomach lurch. This was going to be more difficult than he had anticipated. *Perhaps it would work. Worth a try.* He switched on the ignition and coasted down the hill before engaging the gears and gas.

It is definitely worth a try. Anything is better than just sitting here watching. It made him feel helpless. What if something happened in that house to his little girl? What could he do sitting on his rear out here on the road? He clenched his hands on the steering wheel and glared. He understood Fowler's reasoning, but not when it came to a stubborn little girl who went her own way and was too naïve to sense danger.

"It went well, Gany." Cheryl stroked the feathers on the parrot and then filled its food dish. "There were no gun-carrying thugs that I could see. I only chatted with Francine for a few minutes. Otherwise we got most of the hardscape in place and quite a few of the trees and shrubs."

"Awk. All the world's a stage."

Cheryl had to laugh. Her Nana was fond of Shakespeare and often quoted from his plays as she worked around the house. Although she had given up trying to explain to David Larkin that the parrot's name was Ganymede, alternatively Rosalind, from the play, *As You Like It*, he refused to call the majestic bird anything but Polly and insisted she needed a cracker.

"Awk. Naughty Boy. Naughty Boy."

Cheryl turned in time to see David walking through the front door of the shop. Gany had never forgiven or forgotten the teasing she had gotten from the mischievous teenager next door. She flew off her perch and into her large cage, plucking at the door until it shut behind her.

I should pay attention. That bird has more sense than I do. Cheryl turned to greet David with a bland smile.

"What can I do for you, Detective? Was that your car I glimpsed down by the road today?" She took a deep breath as he loomed over her. She refused to move closer to inhale his scent as she would dearly like to do. That fragrant, spicy shaving lotion had been a part of him since as a teenager he had bungled his first shave. Now she suspected he had to shave twice a day to keep his face from becoming scruffy. The thought of that rough cheek next to hers had her drawing a deep breath.

"What can you do for me?" His face went from a smile to a wicked grin to an outright leer. "Now that's a topic for later tonight. Lots of chatting about that for sure, sweet thing. But I need to discuss your police work for now."

"I'm not doing police work. I merely agreed to identify Mr. Toledo's guests if they arrived while I am working. Police work is what you do. I design gardens," she said firmly as she rearranged some garden folders on the counter.

"*Awk, awk!* Naughty boy! Don't slam the door." The parrot shifted restlessly in her cage and plucked at a bell hanging there, clearly disturbed by the detective's visit.

"Awww, Polly want a cracker?" Larkin walked over and tapped on the side of the cage.

The parrot tucked its head underneath its wings.

"There, I got her quiet now," he said.

Cheryl couldn't contain her smile. "She's got your number, David." Her chuckles tumbled out, and Larkin paused to consider her with renewed concentrated interest. He drew closer and reached for her across the counter. Cheryl, still laughing, darted out of his reach.

"Now I remember you," he said, his voice dropping into the sexy range. "You're that little girl next door and you're all grown up now." He started around the counter but paused when Cheryl stopped laughing and frowned at him.

"Okay, okay. I'll behave. Now listen. First of all, don't look for me when you're on the job. I may or may not be around, but if you look for me, it could call attention, and then we'll both be in the suds.

"Second, it might not be me. You don't know all the policemen and detectives in the police department, but they know to keep a watch on you. Just trust me that you're being monitored at all times when you're at Toledo's. We want you to relax and just be yourself, which is a sweet thing indeed. Not that you need to be sweet to that sleaze ball Toledo."

"It's difficult to relax, but I can forget all this police/ criminal stuff when I get into my work. I'll try my best. Was that you down by the road today?"

"Yes, for a while. Now remember what I said. Don't look for me and if you do see me, don't recognize me. For heaven's sake, don't talk to me. Hopefully all this will be over soon. I gotta go. You wanna come over to my house tonight for pizza?"

"Actually I have a date tonight. A dinner date. But I'll take a rain check on the pizza." She closed her book and tidied the counter. "Thanks for the information. Good luck tomorrow." She gave him a dismissal smile as he stood rooted to the floor.

Finally, he turned without a word and left the shop.

Cheryl leaned across the counter in relief. Larkin was getting harder and harder to handle. Or was it her hormones that were acting up? Difficult to tell at this point. Something or someone was certainly straining her ability to control herself. *A dinner date is just what I need. Mom and Dad do qualify, I think. Who knows whom I'll run into at the country club dining room? I hope not Gordon.*

She punched in a number on her cell. "Mom? Are you and Dad going to be at dinner tonight at the Club? . . . May I join you? . . . Great. What time? . . . Okay, around six it is. See you later." Still short of breath, which seemed to be a perpetual status whenever the huge detective was around, Cheryl went around the corner to cover the parrot's cage.

"Sorry, Gany, he really doesn't mean to upset you anymore. He's just oblivious to what to do and what not to do around a sensitive bird. He sort of grows on you if you relax and let him. Which I'm certainly not going to be doing any time in the future, and forget that I mentioned it, will you? 'Night, 'night now."

"Parting is such sweet *awk*."

Cheryl laughed. "Yes it is, Gany. I'll see you tomorrow." Cheryl could hear the bird settling down on her roost for the night.

She viewed her fingernails. It would take some doing to get them in shape before she met her parents. They loved her but they were baffled by her work. Okay, everyone was baffled because she loved to be outside doing manual labor. She headed for the shower wondering if she'd gotten just a bit too much sun on her nose today. Probably popped out a dozen freckles.

She paused in her appraisal of herself to answer her cell. *Not him again.*

"Hello, Gordon . . . No, I was just about to get into the shower. What's up? . . . Not tonight. I have plans. . . . No, with Mom and Dad. . . . I'm meeting them at the Club. Haven't seen them in a week or two. . . . Well, if you do, make it around dessert time. I have some private things I want to share with my parents, if you don't mind . . ."

"Gordon, I don't want to hurt your feelings, but you do remember we're no longer engaged, don't you?" She listened to his protests.

"Of course, we're friends. Just because I want to have some privacy with my parents doesn't mean I don't want to be your friend. I have to go. . . . Yes, right now. Good-bye, Gordon."

"Can I go to the shower now, do you think?" she asked the heavens above. "I'm determined to get to the shower. Will Gordon never stop being a pest? You'd think he would have figured out he can't control me when I finally broke off the engagement."

David Larkin was making the very same mistake. Admittedly, she was oversensitive to being ordered about, but she would hold firm. No man was ever going to get away with treating her like a brainless minion. Her father had never been guilty of that obnoxious male trait and darned if she'd put up with it from a contemporary—no matter how sexy. He'd treat her with respect or . . .

She stared solemnly at her reflection in the mirror. "Definitely too much sun. Here come the freckles. Big as quarters. No doubt I'll hear about this from a lot of people."

She shook her head regretfully and stepped into her shower. With the hot water streaming over her shoulders and wet head, she closed her eyes and let her thoughts slip wherever they would. Soft brown eyes, sultry voice, hot kisses raining down on her face. She used her washcloth to slowly suds herself. The grime from her work was sliding off along with the worries of the day. Flashes of herself in the garden with David raced through her mind hot with passion and temptation.

Then she laughed. The sound of his surprise when he fell over the statue Pan was too good. The splashing around in the goldfish pool wasn't bad either.

David was going to learn he couldn't indulge his every whim where she was concerned. She was determined to teach him to respect her and her work. Not to mention her person which he seemed to think he could touch, fondle, and kiss whenever the notion stuck him. Never mind that she'd loved every minute of it. That wasn't the point. Or maybe it was.

Chapter 7

Bugs, Salad Greens, and Fun in the Garden
By Cheryl

Everyone should by now be aware of the danger of the careless use of chemicals in the garden. My humble opinion is that heavy pesticides are best left to the farmers who are trained to control the critters who invade our food source. For instance, it's fairly easy to capture those shiny black Japanese beetles without using a single obnoxious pesticide. Go into the garden in the evening just as the sun is setting.

For some reason the beetles are asleep or have fallen into a stupor. Use a coffee can with a bit of water in the bottom and a plastic lid to clap on. Hold the can underneath the largest wad of bugs and tap the plant gently. They'll fall right into your can. Close with the lid and slushy around until they are wet. Keep doing this over and over in the evenings. Not this year, but perhaps by the next or the next, you'll start to see less and less of the annoying critters with nary a pesticide in sight.

Alternately, there are commercial organic preparations to apply to your lawn which disturbs the life cycle of the beetles. If you insist on using the plastic lures, place them in the way back corner of your garden—preferably in your neighbor's backyard, even better, down the street in the vacant lot where your kids play sand lot softball.

Some of you are wondering how to enjoy those crisp greens, which are so easy to grow in your own garden.

Cheryl tapped her foot impatiently. The volleyball game

was on again next door and the grunts and shouts of triumph were distracting. She expected the ball to fly over the hedge any minute now. She was ahead on her column and the job at Toledo's was coming along nicely. What could go wrong?

Something for sure. Her experience was that with David Larkin in the vicinity, anything at all could explode into confusion, mayhem, or kissing. Or all three. Cheryl wasn't certain which was worse. Or more wonderful. She hunched her back, feeling as if both grandmothers were looking over her shoulder.

Sitting in her garden enjoying the last of the sun, she reviewed in her head the next steps to take in the elaborate plans for a two-acre landscaping design. She wanted to go over the list of perennials with Francine. Her plan was to give the client choices, but safe ones. Success in the completion of a beautiful garden was the goal, but she wanted satisfied clients in the process.

She was pleased with the hillside planting. It looked as if it had always been there with the carefully placed boulders and trees. Since money was no object, she was able to move larger trees and shrubbery into the natural terrain. Next came a discreet patio halfway down the slope. She considered should she use natural sandstone pavers. Her patio planters would brighten up the newly purchased metal and mesh table and chairs. Francine said the delivery would be in a couple of days. Cheryl knew she should be ready by then.

She became aware of the silence next door. *Game over?* She had mixed emotions about that. The quiet was nice, but it meant that David was on the loose again. She'd bet her last pair of clippers that . . .

"Cher?" David spoke quietly though the hedge. "You there?"

"I'm here. What's happening?" She closed her laptop and tugged on the neck of her T-shirt. She reached for her glass of ice tea and waited for David. She looked up in surprise when not only David Larkin, but three more burly men trailed through the hedge with him.

"I wanted to introduce you to my friends, Cher. This is Bob, Tony, and Malcolm."

The men, drenched in sweat and wet T-shirts, grinned, wiped their hands on their shorts, and reached forward to shake her hand.

"Sorry we disturbed you the other day," Bob said. "We get a little too enthusiastic occasionally. Ole Dave here has mentioned how nice your garden is. Hope we don't harm it again."

"That's right. We told Dave to pull up on that wild overhead smash of his. No good will come of it anyway," Tony said with a sideways smirk at David.

Malcolm just smiled and said nothing.

Stunned, Cheryl floundered, trying to think of what to say to four hulking men all standing respectively in front of her and grinning. Finally, she managed to find a semi-gracious response.

"Thank you for your concern. It was only one lily. I barely heard you today. Are you all with the police department like David?"

They nodded.

"You look so familiar," she said to Malcolm.

He dipped his head sheepishly. "I was with Dave the other night when we rescued you and your friend in the old garden. How is she, by the way?"

She answered his grin with one of her own. "Jane? She's fine. Refuses to go with me back to retrieve my spade and basket however."

"Probably not a bad idea. One of the boys can get them for you. Best if you and Jane, is it?, allow us to do it. Safer, you know."

"I'm one of the crew assigned to look out for you, ma'am. I'll be working for the landscaper. I'd appreciate it if you would pretend you don't know me. It would help me do my job." He relaxed with his hands clasped in front of him with David watching with a half-smile on his face.

Cheryl smiled back at Malcolm and nodded. In truth, she was floored to learn of the heavy involvement of the police department in this project. Did she feel safer or more afraid? The situation was far more serious than she'd first thought.

"Must say, if you don't take offense, I really like what you are doing up there on that barren hill. The change is beautiful. Looks like it was always growing there."

David then took over and hustled the men off the property. Cheryl sat waiting for him with the new information to digest.

When he returned, he trailed his fingers across her back, wrapping his hand around her neck, making chills run up and down her arms. Fumes of sweat and maleness wafted across the garden toward her mixing with the sweet fragrance of four o'clocks. David flopped down on the grass beside her chair, perspiration still rolling down his face. He reached for a bandana from his shorts' pocket.

"Did we disturb you today? I still feel guilty about your plant. Did you get another? I'll be happy to pay for it." He grinned beguilingly up at her, his hair soaked and curling around his ears. She found herself smiling back. He could be so sweet when he wanted—sexy, sexy, sexy. If she was full of sweat and dirt with soaked clothes, even her mother wouldn't come near her. It just wasn't fair. Men could get away with anything.

"It's okay, David. There isn't another, but you didn't kill it. Just stopped the bloom for this year. It'll be back next year, but thanks for the thought."

He frowned, looking down at his disreputable sneakers. "It was something really special to you, wasn't it? I swear it really was an accident. Let me do something nice. Can I take you out to dinner? I know you probably have dates that do that, but you and I are old friends. We can go out occasionally, can't we? Or I can cook for you. You won't believe it, but I'm not a bad cook." He patted her on the knee, and she braced for further liberties.

"I promise to behave, Cher. Don't be mad at me for the other night. You were so cute I couldn't help myself. We've known each other so long I thought . . . well, never mind what I thought. But listen, about that dinner? You aren't going steady with anyone, are you?"

She ignored his rapid-fire questions wondering why he seemed nervous. *What's up?* "Mom and Dad said to say hello to you and to tell you they were surprised that you decided to keep your grandmother's house. I saw them the other night at dinner."

"Did you? They are well? I can't remember the last time I saw them. Was it? Yes, at the funeral. Good people, your folks. Not a bit like your grandmother, but very nice people." He was quiet and looked thoughtful for a moment.

Cheryl allowed the peace of the garden to seep into her shoulders. It was nice sitting here with David when he wasn't destroying her gardens. He seemed to be comfortable with her as well.

"Pretty," he said, staring at the colorful flowers. "Cute little birds fluttering around those nice-smelling plants. What are they?" He wiped his forehead again.

"The flowers are called four o'clocks. I guess because they only open in the late evening. Hummingbirds love them. That tiny one over there isn't really a bird. He's a look-alike moth, called a Sphinx or a hawk moth. A fake, as it were. He only pretends to be a bird." She lifted her eyebrows at him significantly.

"What? I'm really a cop, I swear. Just because I don't wear a uniform . . . Oh, you're kidding me."

"Your friends seem very nice, David. Thank you for introducing them to me."

"They're good fellows. Give me a hard time, but I'd trust them to watch my back any time. They have families, well, two of them do. Malcolm is still holding out. Think he's got a thing for Jane? I heard him perk up when he found out her name."

"She hasn't mentioned anything to me. She's just getting over a bad relationship and may not be responsive to any overtures. I had almost forgotten about him being with you that night. He seems very nice."

"Ah, well. I didn't want you to think we are all 'beasts' like me." He abruptly stood, towering over her. "I need a shower bad. You gonna have dinner with me? You choose where and when." With his long stride, he rounded the opening in the hedge before she could make up her mind to answer him.

Did she want to have dinner with David? Perhaps that would be a good idea. If they could normalize the fact that they were neighbors and allow ordinary days to happen, then just maybe. It was her only hope. The man was invading her dreams and haunting her days.

David had gotten a job as a day laborer with the landscaper who was still working on the other side of the slope. She had been startled almost out of her hard hat when David looked straight up at her and winked. She knew her face had flushed, but Francine was already leaving. She was enthusiastically making shopping plans to buy the new patio furniture. Cheryl found herself in awe how that woman could navigate in those spike heels all through the mud and grass.

Cheryl blew out a breath. She couldn't make up her mind whether having David that close was a good thing or not. For some reason she was pleased he could see her at her work. On the other hand, he was almost more distraction than she could handle. David Larkin in a tight T-shirt with his muscles bulging could distract a nun. And she was no nun.

There had been no visitors since she had started work on the Toledo property. What she was supposed to report on she had no idea. She had almost forgotten about it when she spotted David swinging a shovel like he was born to dig. He ducked his head and stayed out of sight when Sam Toledo stood at the top of the terrace surveying the ongoing work. So far, Cheryl had dealt only with Francine, and she sincerely hoped it would stay that way. If there were to be visitors, she assumed they would come next week to the big party.

Dinner? Okay, perhaps it would be fun. A new Mexican restaurant had opened up a couple of blocks over. They could walk. It was a nice night. She gathered her things together and went inside. *Finish the column tomorrow evening. I swear I will.*

She prowled through her dresser drawer looking for the blue blouse that matched her eyes. Just slacks and sandals. Nothing fancy. Gold bracelet. Tiny earrings. That's okay, she thought. Why she was bothering with a dab of perfume behind her ears, she had no idea. She ran a comb through her curls and called it good enough. She had never fussed with her hair and she wasn't about to start now. Her natural curls would stay fairly neat if she kept them trimmed. She grabbed the ringing phone deciding to tell David she was ready to go now.

Gordon. Damn. Damn and double damn. That man just wouldn't take no for an answer. She was still irritated about the other night when he sat down at the table at the club, greeting her parents with a kiss for her mother and a warm handshake for her dad. As if he was a member of the family. That engagement had ended over a year ago, but he just wouldn't accept it. Her mother was still giving her a sorrowful look whenever the subject of the doctor came up. What mother didn't want her daughter to marry a doctor? It was an embarrassing cliché.

Gordon Moore was known as dermatologist extraordinaire. He was good looking and very comfortably fixed with more patients than he could handle, with the annoying habit of thinking he could control Cheryl's every thought and action. It wasn't a fault that was apparent at the beginning of the relationship, but after she accepted the ring, it doubled in intensity.

He called her at work. He insisted she be available to him no matter what her plans. She certainly had no intentions of becoming merely an appendage to a man no matter how eligible he was rated. She ended the relationship as quickly as she could. Her parents were shocked. Gordon was wrong in thinking the break was temporary.

"No, I'm sorry, Gordon. I do have plans for dinner. Not to mention that I've worked hard all day and I'm very tired. No, I don't want to make plans to see you any time soon. Listen, Gordon." She peered out the window to check for David. "I have to go. You have a nice evening. Bye." She clicked off just as David knocked on the back door. Wow. He knocked for a change. Almost civilized. Cheryl wondered what had changed his mind.

"You ready, sweetheart? What did you decide, sexy lady? That blouse is exactly the same color of your big blue eyes. You don't need boosting into my tree house, do you?" He chuckled.

Understanding the reference, she laughed. "Mexican suit you? There's a new one over on Elm. It's a nice night. We could walk."

He nodded and reached for her hand. She felt his large fingers wrapping around hers, engulfing them. A satisfied, safe feeling came over her, and she smiled up at him. Home. Why did she feel as if she had come home?

Silly Cheryl. You are falling under the spell of David Gillard Larkin once more. Tonight he's the handsome Irishman with a mouth full of sweet blarney.

They swung their hands and bumped shoulders as they walked into the growing darkness. It was a pleasant night with little traffic and almost no wind. Most folks were at home eating dinner. As they crossed the street, David rested a hand in the middle of her back and reached across to hold her hand with his other one.

I'm protected from the absolute world, she thought. Nothing bad can ever happen to me when I am with this man. I've been in love with him for half my life and I sincerely hope he never finds out.

Her grandmother had said he had growing up to do before he would be ready for a real relationship. She never said how many years it would take, but sometimes Cheryl would get tantalizing glimpses of the man he could be.

Cheryl suppressed her feelings as best she could. Her heart was still in serious danger with this man until she could find a way to make him ordinary. He had broken her young teenage heart with a casual promise not kept, but eventually she had recovered. She had gotten over it, but never had she forgotten her disappointment.

David could destroy her if she wasn't careful and it would only be her fault. She was certain she knew him—what he was and what he wasn't.

David had many holes in her expectations for a perfect mate. He was never going to qualify as a candidate for a lifetime partner. Was she even in the market for a permanent relationship? His eye was ever roving for one thing. Yes, she knew he was fond of her, but fondness did not hold up to a full-time commitment.

Her grandmother had promised one day David Larkin would grow up and be less callused toward her feelings.

"Young men are pretty self-serving, Cheryl. They need a few years on them before they can see others."

Cheryl was afraid David would never see her as anything other than the tagalong next-door neighbor she had once been. He would protect her and fight anyone who abused her like the football player on prom night, meanwhile stealing a kiss for himself without a thought to her feelings.

She sighed. What a dilemma.

Chapter 8

Okay, Cheryl admitted to herself, David Larkin was pretty special. She wasn't the only female who felt that way, and she was acutely aware of it. She was supposed to be working on her account books, but the pouring rain outside was giving her the day off. There was just too much mud to continue the work, and she needed the precious time to catch up on other jobs and paperwork. Besides, they were way ahead of where she expected to be. Even Francine had commented on the efficiency of the workers. Did that have anything to do with David?

She scoffed. He couldn't arrange all that.

Okay, she agreed he was a pretty special fellow, but he wasn't the president or anything. Be hard to think otherwise after that fiasco at dinner the other night. She had chosen the restaurant so she couldn't blame the waitress's behavior on David.

She was all over him, hanging those plastic breasts practically on his nose. Cheryl thought at first it was an old girlfriend, or a current one, but no. David, to give him credit, didn't encourage the pushy woman, but he grinned later, leaning over and winking at Cheryl. "Think she likes me?"

Cheryl had acerbically replied that it was probably the tip she liked. But to be honest, she knew better. Big David Larkin, Detective extraordinary at the Hubbard Police Department, was a virile, good-looking male, and the ladies knew it. Some merely cut their eyes as he walked by and some, like the waitress, were brazen enough to flirt right in front of his date. They all treated him like so much male eye candy. It was no wonder David had a difficult time settling down. It must be hard to choose just one piece when you're let loose in a candy store.

Cheryl reminded herself to steel her resolve against ole Eye Candy Man himself. No way was she going to enter the competition, history between them or not. It was already difficult enough just going through with this 'let's be friends' kick David seemed to be on.

Remember who he is, Cheryl. David Larkin, Hedge Hopper, Plant Killer, and breaker of little girl's hearts. As fascinating as he was, Cheryl knew that eventually, if she allowed herself to be drawn into the vortex that was David, disaster would happen. It always had and Cheryl would historically be too intrigued to resist.

Not this doggone time. She looked up as the bell on the door tingled and the parrot shifted on her perch and squawked, "Come in, come in. The door is open."

A young couple entered the shop. The attractive redheaded woman was wearing tailored linen pants and a silk shirt with the sleeves rolled up. Her young executive-type escort sported a blue blazer and charcoal slacks which shouted new money. Both owned expensive orthodontist smiles.

"Hi, welcome to Garden Design for You. I'm Cheryl. How can I help you?"

"Hi, I'm Betts. This is my husband, Jack Malone. We know your parents from the country club."

They each smiled broadly as if they knew a secret and Cheryl didn't.

"That's nice." Cheryl politely waited for more information. She had a bad feeling about this couple.

"We were chatting with your folks at the buffet the other night, and they thought you would be able to help us with a unique problem."

Again flashed the dazzling smiles.

"I will certainly try my best. Could you give me a short outline of the task?" Cheryl almost hoped it was out of her league. She had enough on her hands right at the moment.

"Well." Jack's face flushed slightly. "I play a little golf, but my game isn't all that great." He tugged at his collar, and Betts patted him reassuringly. He grabbed her hand.

"Can you design a golf course with a few holes and a putting green for my backyard?" he asked all in a rush.

Back came the grins. Cheryl decided the smiles were to cover uncertainly and embarrassments and she warmed a bit.

"Certainly I can design a golf course, but how big is your backyard? There are limitations to what I can accomplish without acreage, you know."

A golf course! Now that was a new one for her. What on earth had her parents gotten her into this time? Bad enough her mother kept encouraging her ex-fiancé. Cheryl could enlighten her that marrying a doctor was only a cliché if she'd listen. She put aside her musings and concentrated on setting the couple at ease.

"We own about five acres but the sub division has restrictions on yard design. We wondered if you could disguise it as gardens. Perhaps with some casual screening from the street to give us a bit more privacy? It could be compact. Just a few holes and a putting green?"

"It would be a challenge, but wouldn't it be easier for you to just go to a pro shop and arrange for lessons? This could run into some real money, you know."

The young man flushed. "I can deduct it as a business expense and legitimately too. I entertain VIP clients and they insist on their privacy. Is this something you can do?"

Cheryl was quiet for a moment while the couple waited. It was a strange request. Might be best to consult her lawyer before she went much further. Actually, the situation intrigued her, and she thought she might enjoy the challenge. What was the worst thing that could happen? Her investigation would prove the unsuitability of the project, and she would need to withdraw? That didn't sound so terrible.

"How about I come by to see your property before I commit? Would tomorrow be convenient?" The appointment was arranged, and the couple left with the parrot singing out that parting was such sweet . . . *awkk*.

"Wow. This could run into a large challenge, not to mention I could use the funds. What do you think, Gany? Should I thank Mom and Dad for the vote of confidence? It was certainly a nice surprise to learn they think I could accomplish a project this size. I'm talking to a bird again. Grandmother would laugh, wouldn't she?" Cheryl filled the parrot's food dish with seeds and a chopped-up apple. The parrot murmured approval while tilting its head to one side and eyeing the tastiest morsels before settling down to eat.

If she could work it, she could start this job just as the Toledo one was ending—or meld the two together, phasing one out as the other started up. It might work. She'd need to check out the budget before her head started designing gardens to hide a golf course, even a limited one.

With her imagination firmly in her notebook designing sand traps, Cheryl absently picked up her phone without checking caller ID. And groaned.

"Gordon. Don't you ever work?" She tapped her pen rapidly on the desk. When would he ever give up and leave her in peace?

"No, no, and no." . . . She tried to keep her voice quiet to disguise her rising fury. "Those days are absolutely over. I am working, a fact you failed to respect when we were engaged . . . I certainly will not accompany you on a business trip." She gazed out the window cursing the day she ever met this man.

"I don't much care what you think, Gordon. Our engagement ended almost a year ago, but you seem to be in some sort of time warp. Listen to me carefully." How could she get it across to him? What word selection could she choose that would finally penetrate his closed-off mind?

"I do not want you to call this number again unless you are ordering plants for your garden. And even then, I will refer you to someone else. Our relationship is over and at this point, I'm questioning whether I want to be your friend. Let it go, Gordon. Do yourself a favor and let it go." She listened to his pseudo-calm protestations for a second—she knew he was fuming—but he prided himself on keeping his cool. It was all part and partial of his control issues. He just could not believe a mere woman would dump his bullying behind. Well, she had had it and it was time she got tough enough to convince him.

"Good-bye, Gordon." She hung up the phone in his mid-sentence and slumped across the desk. Immediately the phone rang again and she glared at it before finally picking it up.

"I told you not to call this number again! If you keep this up I'll . . ."

Jane was sputtering on the other end of the line.

"Oh, I thought you were that maddening ex-fiancé of mine," Cheryl interrupted her. "He keeps on acting as if I hadn't broken the engagement months ago." . . . She closed her bankbook.

"I know! It's exactly why I did break off the relationship. He just sees people as something he controls. He manipulates to get what he wants and doesn't consider the other person's feelings at all. Probably thinks I'm one of his employees who must do what he says without question." . . . She glanced at the clock. Her free rain day was rapidly coming to a close and she hadn't gotten half the work done she had intended.

"Pizza? Sure, but could you bring it over here? I still have work to do and if I leave . . . right. Around an hour from now? Pepperoni and mushrooms, oh, and green peppers and olives, sausages if you like them. Thanks, friend. You've cheered me up. See you in a little bit."

Cheryl hung up and turned to the parrot. "You about ready to retire, Gany? It's been a busy day in spite of the weather, hasn't it?" Cheryl knew she sounded just like her nana, talking to a bird as if she could understand. She pulled the cover over the cage and turned out the lights.

"Just time for a few words on my column. What shall I write about this week?" She sat down at the kitchen table and opened her laptop.

"Shopping for your Plants"
by Cheryl

There are many places to obtain plants for your garden. Local nurseries are probably the number one choice. You can inspect the merchandise on the spot. The nurseryman can answer any questions you have about the plant, including the particular zone it thrives in best. Know your local agricultural zone. A plant can be gorgeous during the summer, but unless it is winter hardy to your area, you are not likely to see it another year. Think Florida and then Maine. The plantings would need different requirements: Florida flora must withstand the heat, whereas Maine plants should stand up to harsh winters. Most local nurserymen are ethical and will notify you of the plant's hardiness. This is not always true about the plant sections of the box stores.

For one thing, the clerks might not know. They are taught to water the plants and to service the checkout counter. Plant people they may not be. The lower price could be tempting, but what you gain in bargain hunting may be lost when your plant fails to thrive.

Form a relationship with the person you buy your plants from the same as you would in any other professional relationship, with the exception of those people who absolutely insist on nursing a sick plant back to health or playing hospice to the ones who die. Another word of caution, examine the plant carefully before you purchase. Look for diseased leaves and pest that may be lurking. One ill plant could infect your entire garden.

Farmers' markets and neighbors are two good sources for plants. Farmers who bring their merchandize to market are local citizens. They know the zone and the conditions of the area. Neighbors who garden need a place to unload excess perennials which have been split. Lucky you if you have a neighbor like that.

A knock on the door made her pause but she didn't turn around. She needed to finish the column.

"Come on in, Jane." She kept working and jumped when a kiss and scratchy beard landed on her bare neck. David. She looked up and held his gaze. She could see immediately that he was tired, wet, and upset. He slide into the chair beside hers and put his head on the table.

"I need you, Cheryl. Please?"

She closed her laptop and rose to stand behind him. "Who helped you when you were away?" she asked as she kneaded his shoulders and massaged his neck. He groaned in ecstasy as she dug into the tense muscles.

"No one ever could help me like you do, little Cher. You have the magic fingers of a saint. Ahhh, just a little to the right."

"What's got you upset? I can see you are in a twist about something. Come on, out with it." She tugged his ear gently and ran her fingers through his thick hair.

"Can't tell you. Some things are best left unsaid, but I can attest to the fact that there is no limit to what man can do to man. Some sort of quote there, I think, but it's true. And disgusting. It gave me a major headache. You know how I feel when it concerns young people."

He straightened up and shrugged his massive shoulders back and forth. Then he reached for her hand. "You are the sweetest, Cher. It feels so much better. Did I hear you say Jane was coming over?"

"Yep, and I hope she'll have enough food for you too. How about I make a salad to round it out? Why don't you go into the bathroom and towel off until the pizza gets here? She might have wings too."

He nodded but leaned over to kiss her on top her head while holding her to him briefly. Cheryl leaned her head against his chest and made no protest. He was harmless when his stress headache was acting up. Tension could and often did trigger it. He'd suffered with them since puberty.

As he left the room, Jane entered the back door laden with food. She did indeed have Buffalo wings as well as a large pizza. David must have sniffed it out. She dropped it all on the table and collapsed into a kitchen chair.

"Whew. That rain is fierce. Could hardly see to drive that last mile. Do we need to build an ark? What're you making? I thought I'd covered all the bases. Oh."

Jane stared, and her mouth dropped open as David, partially wrapped in a blanket, came bare-chested into the room.

"Oh my," she said. "You're here. Hello, David. How are you?" She started to babble staring at the tangle of black hair on his chest which arrowed down in an intriguing v and disappeared into a pair of well-fitted jeans.

Cheryl turned away. She couldn't blame Jane. David was a spectacular sight. Cheryl had to busy herself to maintain her own calm balance at the sight of the partially naked detective.

"Can I dry your shirt, David?" she asked without turning around. She waited until he handed it to her then hurried to the back utility room. She leaned over the washing machine and took a deep breath.

Opening the dryer, she thrust his shirt inside, acutely aware of the familiar scent of David.

Concentrate on the pizza, she chided her rampant libido, hoping it would subside. Her vulnerabilities to this man were getting out of control. Why didn't an immune set up the more she saw of him instead of a reaction the other way? A chemical bonding must have happened when she was otherwise occupied. Now she couldn't shake it loose. Had she really tried? Really? She shook herself and reentered the room. Thank goodness the fragrance of a well-made pizza filled the kitchen, blocking out any other tempting aromas.

Chapter 9

With Jane riding shotgun, Cheryl turned into the gated subdivision and started calling out street names. An invading army would never find their way around this place, Cheryl thought. Perhaps this was in the planner's mind when he laid out the initial design.

The homes were widely spaced with trees shading acres of well-kept lawn with foundation plantings, but with her expert eye, Cheryl could see few perennial gardens. Did her clients know their plans would stand their grounds out in a neighborhood that kept actual gardening to a minimum? *Not my problem, but I will warn them in advance of any actual work.*

The house was large, about ten years old and to her critical eye, boring. And expensive. This couple was on the way up the corporate ladder. Not much to change. The acreage in back seemed to consist of scrub brush, first forestation, and native trees. The front was a sculptured lawn probably maintained by a service. Although the recent rain was helping, it was obvious the lawn suffered from heat, lack of water, and too many close mows. The service liked its money. A sprinkling system would have been an asset.

She wished the rain had actually stopped. The sun tried, but according to the weather report, bands of rain showers would continue to sweep the area at least through today. Jane and she were suitably decked out to walk the grounds, rain or shine, but it was always more pleasant to explore in dry weather. A phone call had alerted Betts, and she met them at the door.

"What can I get you? Tea? Coffee?" Her smile was almost blinding, but now Cheryl understood it was her way of chasing nerves.

She kept shaking her head no. "We just need access to your back acreage. I wouldn't want the neighbors to call the police if they saw us. How about I stop back by here before we leave? By the way, this is my friend, Jane Stewart. She works with me."

The two exchanged pleasantries and Cheryl headed for the back door. She wanted to get back to the Toledo job if the rain stopped long enough for the equipment to get in. *This shouldn't take very long.*

Cheryl was pleased her initial assessment was correct. This land was practically a blank canvas in spite of the beauty of the wild flowers that grew there. Most of the growth could be scraped out without any trouble. Shifting her eyes toward what she thought might be the very back of the lot, she could see the neighbor directly behind had a line of evergreens no doubt marking the property line. One good-sized oak tree beckoned her forward. They would make sure to save it. It was a sin to destroy a valuable hardwood tree that took so many years to grow.

Jane wandered off calling out that she had spotted wild black berries. Cheryl neared the oak and stared up into the branches admiring the strong, healthy specimen. The ground underneath and around the tree was barren, naked hard-packed earth, either from lack of water or from frequent picnic visitors in the past.

The wind puffed moisture-laden air toward her and she wrinkled her nose in distaste. She walked around the tree expecting to find an animal carcass, but it was a person instead, sitting upright leaning his head against the oak tree.

Dead. Very dead. Bugs were crawling out of places Cheryl didn't want to contemplate. With a great deal of effort, she suppressed a scream. Hands shaking, she reached into her pocket for her cell and dialed 911. After she completed the call, she called out to her friend.

"Jane, can you come over here for a second?" She'd send Jane to inform Betts that the police would soon be arriving.

"Why are the police coming?" Jane asked. "What did we do wrong this time?"

Cheryl explained but recommended to Jane not to look around the tree.

"It's not a pretty sight. You'd be better off not knowing." Nausea rose up, and Cheryl felt slightly dizzy. The dank odor tickled her nose and she swallowed rapidly trying to control her senses. "I wish I hadn't seen the poor man myself."

"Okay. I'll take your word for it. I'll wait for you at the Malone's house, all right?" She trudged through the brush, glancing back at Cheryl a time or two, her face a study in confusion with a smear of berry juice on her lips.

Cheryl shifted slightly to glance behind and spotted a shoe entangled in a short patch of wild St. John's wort. She wasn't certain it belonged to the dead man. She hadn't noticed if he had on both his shoes. Then belatedly she remembered she shouldn't be contaminating a crime scene and moved back to the safe side of the oak. In the distance, she heard the whine of police sirens. She breathed a sigh of relief. This was not a problem for her to solve.

When David arrived, she was standing alone out in the street. He jumped out of his car and gathered her firmly to him. For once, she relaxed and let herself be completely engulfed by those protective arms. They had been there for her when she was a frightened young girl and there for her now. Safe.

She needed to feel safe. The familiar smell of David surrounded her, and she snuggled her head on his chest, oblivious to the poke of a gun holster into her shoulder. He murmured soft words and squeezed her, comforting her as if she were still that ten-year-old who fell out of the apple tree.

"You okay, Cher? You'll be just fine in a little bit. It's upsetting to see violence like that. I know, honey. I know." He cuddled her for a moment, leaning against her car.

Finally, she lifted her head. "I found one of your men, David. Did they tell you?"

He tucked her head back down on his chest.

"Yeah, baby. They told me. That's how I knew where you were. What were you and Jane doing out there in the first place? How do you know these people?" He released her and they walked a little way toward his car.

"Potential clients. Only met them yesterday. My parents recommended them. They know them from the Country Club." She shuddered, still trying to erase the visual of the dead man behind an oak tree.

David had shifted into full detective mode and gave her a glance that expressed doubt. He wasn't rolling his eyes yet, she thought. Cheryl knew he had always considered the country club crowd snobs, although he respected her parents.

"What were you doing way back there? Weren't the gardens closer to the house?" Still holding her hand firmly, he scanned the area.

Cheryl gulped and swallowed a hysterical giggle. She held tight to David's hand, still needing the comfort of him near her.

"They want me to build them a golf practice area in their backyard." She looked up at him and wondered why she spent so much time pushing him away. His solid chest and shoulders were almost like a barrier between her and a world gone weird.

"They want you to put a putting green in their backyard?" David shook his head. "Are they nuts? This is a restricted neighborhood."

"Yes. I was just making a preliminary inspection of the grounds. I haven't actually accepted the job." She stepped away enough to see David's face. "Who is that man? And who do you think shot him?"

"Well, you might have guessed he was a friend of Toledo's. Yes, he's one of the men in the photos we gave you, not from around here, but he was expected to show up in the area. Just not dead. This complicates the case."

They stood silent for a minute, still holding hands, until Jane appeared leaving by the front door of the Malone's house and started down the drive toward them. Cheryl let go of David's hand. He tilted her chin up, inspecting her eyes and face critically.

"You gonna be all right? You want me to drive you home?"

With all my heart! "No, Jane and I have other things we need to be doing this morning. Do you think you can come over tonight and tell me more about all this?"

He nodded but Cheryl could see he was distracted. He reached for his cell in the holder at his belt. Still murmuring into the phone, he pulled her to him from the nape of her neck. He planted a quick but firm kiss on her lips and strolled toward the black-and-white parked up the street. As he left, he was still concentrating on the phone conversation.

Jane gave a huge sigh as she climbed into Cheryl's car. "I swear. Life with you is never dull. All the adventures we've had never included a dead body before. Who do you think that man was? Some burglar? What was he doing way back there?" She buckled her seat belt as Cheryl pulled swiftly out into traffic.

"I dunno to all your questions. Can we just concentrate on getting the heck out of here right now? David promised to come over tonight and give me more information. I'll let you know as soon as I find out. I knew the minute I saw that couple there would be trouble. Some sort of premonition, don't really know why. They seem nice enough, and it wasn't their fault some man decided to die right there underneath their tree." Cheryl couldn't stop herself from shuddering. She wondered how long it would be before she stopped seeing that blank stare. "I hope I don't dream about it."

"Do you think he just sat down underneath the tree like Rip Van Winkle and went to sleep never to wake up?" Jane was obviously still mulling over the incident.

"He went to sleep, all right. He had a couple of holes in his forehead. Someone shot him." Cheryl tried to suppress the memory.

"He was murdered! You didn't tell me he was murdered. Oh, my. I can't believe we found a murdered man. Did you tell David about that?" She wrung her hands in excitement.

"Yes, he knew. The uniform cops radioed him. He's one of the detectives who will work on the case, probably. You want to go to lunch at my parents' house? I could use some petting. How about you?"

Jane nodded enthusiastically. She knew the Esterbrooks would feed them well.

"This day is turning out to be a big surprise all around, isn't it?" Jane asked. "First, we find a dead man, then we find out he's murdered, then we get to have a special lunch with your parents. Wonder what the rest of the day will be like," Jane said, giggling, only slightly hysterically.

"Did I tell you that I met the policeman who dragged you out of the old garden the other night? He asked about you. Nice-looking fellow." Cheryl glanced sideways and saw Jane's jaw drop.

"No, really, Cheryl? The big fellow? He kept apologizing for holding his hand over my mouth. Smelled like mint chocolate. He asked about me? What was his name?"

"Malcolm. I don't know the rest. He plays volleyball with David, one of those noisy ones that come over. David invited them to meet me. They all apologized for the poor lily that was smashed."

"He was cute. Do you suppose?" Jane subsided into thoughtful silence, which was Cheryl's intent. She didn't want to answer any more questions about the dead man.

Cheryl intended to quiz her parents about the Malone's, but she kept quiet on that subject for now. No sense in alarming Jane more than she had to. Life was complicated enough as it was.

The Esterbrooks were just going out to the Country Club for lunch and insisted that Cheryl and Jane join them. Cheryl forgot how dependent they were on the dining room at their club. Just what they wanted to chat about over an elegant lunch. Who killed a man and dumped him on the Malone's property? No, that wasn't it. How did it happen that they'd recommended the Malone's to Cheryl in the first place and had they any knowledge of their background?

Jane preempted her, of course. "You won't believe what happened to us this morning," she rattled off in a too loud voice. Cheryl tried to poke her underneath the table, but to no avail. "Oh, sorry." Jane smiled at Cheryl and scooted her chair over a bit.

"We went over to look at that backyard acreage . . . ouch!" She turned a wounded face to Cheryl. "Oh, okay. You wanted to tell your parents, didn't you? I'll keep quiet. See, I'm zipping my lips. I won't say a word about what you found under the tree."

"Too late. The beans are spilled. Tell all, daughter," her father ordered.

Her mother's eyes crinkled with worry while guilt raced through Cheryl's stomach. She hated upsetting her mother.

"What happened?" her mother asked. "I worry about you off by yourself. You had Jane with you, though. Still, I just don't know why you didn't take over your father's office. You got that business degree." She rearranged the silverware beside her plate so that it was perfectly aligned. "It was so right for you."

"Nothing exactly happened to me," Cher explained. "I did want to ask you why you recommended me to the Malone's. How well do you know them?" She had their attention now, and both focused on her with intent gazes. Her parents weren't slow turtles. They read between the lines just fine.

"Not very well. We met them about a month ago here at the Club. Seemed a nice enough young couple. He's in finance so I understand. Sounded similar to what my old office dealt in. The company he's affiliated with is respectable, or at least used to be. I'm retired for five years now. Things change. Why do you ask, honey? Did you lose money with them?"

Before Cheryl could reply, her mother rushed to say, "We recommended them to you for your business. We didn't mean for you to be forced to work for them. They talked about a big project. We thought it might give your little business a boost. Did it turn out wrong?" She clasped her hands together.

Her mom's emotions were right out there for the world to see. Her dad was different. He had a pleasant expression turned to the world, but one never knew exactly what he was thinking. He was a 'can do' kind of fellow though. If she had a real problem, she wouldn't hesitate to ask for his counsel. Usually he was very tactful.

"It's kind of a long story," Cheryl hedged. "Can we order first? I'm starving and I'm sure Jane is too.

Everyone agreed, and her dad called for the waiter.

"Unless you want to just eat from the buffet. Alaska salmon is the special."

Cheryl couldn't fathom eating fish of any kind today. In fact, she wasn't sure she could eat anything at all. "I think one of your wonderful hamburgers with sweet-potato fries would suit me just fine," she said.

"It really had nothing to do with me, Dad. I was walking the property and spotted this half-grown oak tree, a lovely specimen. I headed over that way—it sat right on the property line, I think. I wanted to be sure I could save it from the bulldozers."

"Cheryl! Hello! What are you doing here? I thought you had left us and gone to join 'the real work force.' Tired of it already?" She laughed like the hyena she was.

"Hello, Alexia. It's been a long time. How are you?" Cheryl hoped she had inherited some of her father's ability to keep his feelings to himself. Alexia Williams was a high school acquaintance of hers who grew up to be the town crier. She married a geek who kept her in sports cars but seemed to look straight through her whenever they were out together. Cheryl wondered if he even remembered her name.

"I'm just having a quiet lunch with my parents, Alexia. You know how it is. Privacy is hard to come by." Did you have to be hit over the head with a two-by-four? *Go away, Alexia*, Cheryl muttered in her thoughts. Finally the unwanted interruption left.

"Anyway, Dad and Mom, long story short, I found a body behind the tree that sat on the property line. I can't say for sure, but it looked like he'd been shot. I confess I'm a bit shook up about it."

They both exclaimed with horror.

"Did you call the police?"

"What did the police say?"

"Who was it?"

"Did you talk to David Larkin?" her father asked and looked relieved when she nodded yes.

"He came over while we were waiting for the police. He'll probably be on the team that does the investigation."

"You don't think the Malones had anything to do with this corpse, do you?" her father asked. "They seemed totally innocuous when we chatted with them. I'll see what I can find out and call you."

"Fair enough. I have work to do when it stops raining.

"This is that total remake you're doing for Sam Toledo up on the hill, right?" her dad asked. "What did David say about you working up there?"

Cheryl gave him a startled look. "Why should David have anything to say about where I work? Jeepers, Dad. You men think you have the say so over us women. I just got out of a relationship where a man thought he had the right to dictate my every move. You are my father and I respect your opinions, but I'm an adult. As for David . . ."

"Well, look who's here. How are you, Mr. and Mrs. Esterbrook? And Jane. Haven't seen you in ages." Without even glancing at Cheryl's father for permission to join them, Gordon pulled a chair from another table and settled, crowding between her and Jane.

Cheryl remembered belatedly why she disliked dining at the Country Club.

"Don't you think you should have waited to be invited to join our table, Gordon?" Cheryl asked as she looked at her watch and then caught Jane's eye. It was time for them to leave.

Reading the message correctly this time, Jane gathered her purse and murmured her thanks to Cheryl's parents.

"Ha-ha. As if I was a stranger to the family when you know how close we all are. Right, Mrs. Esterbrook?" He looked to her mother for confirmation, but frowned slightly when she remained silent.

"How is retirement, Mr. Esterbrook? Getting any reading done? I'll bet you're enjoying those lazy days of doing nothing."

Her father remained silent as well, and Gordon floundered.

As Cheryl stood and reached for her purse, Gordon jumped up and held her chair for her. She pointedly ignored him and leaned over to kiss her mother's cheek. "I'll see you later, Mom."

"Call me on that research topic, will you, Dad? I'll wait to decide about the new project until I hear from you." Cheryl kissed his cheek then called for her car. Jane and she stood outside waiting for the valet service.

Gordon, who had followed them from the dining room, persistently tried to engage her in conversation.

"I've postponed that business trip until you are free to join me, Cheryl. I know how you love visiting San Francisco." He gave a hearty laugh as if he had said something witty.

Cheryl ignored him totally, while Jane nervously rubbed her eyes.

Relieved when her car was brought around, Cheryl slid behind the wheel while Jane popped in from the other side. Gordon kept a smile on his face.

"He loves you still, Cher," Jane said. "Are you sure you made the right decision. Perhaps you just had a lover's spat and . . . My God, he's a doctor, for goodness' sake! How many chances are you going to get?"

"No. You're wrong, Jane. He never loved me." Cheryl shook her head. "I don't want to talk it. Please. I just wish he would accept that our relationship is dead and buried. Darn. Wish I'd found another word to describe it. Dead isn't my favorite word these days."

"What did David say about the poor man with the holes in his head? Did he say it was a murder?" Jane persisted.

"He really didn't say much at all about it, really. He did promise me details tonight. I can't believe we were the ones to find that man. I only wanted a closer look at the young oak. What did the Malones say when you spoke with them?"

"She didn't seem so upset, but she had no idea it was a murder. They just told her there was a corpse up there and to stay in her house until the police tended to it." Jane turned to her and spoke urgently. "Cheryl, do you think they killed that poor man?"

"No. Emphatically not. I just wanted to know what my father knew about their background. I don't want to take the job if there's anything shady about them. Let's think of more pleasant subjects for the rest of the day, shall we? Surely we can think of something."

"Well, how about how good-looking your next-door neighbor is, and when do you think he will have another volleyball game?" Jane tried for an innocent face but failed.

Chapter 10

The rains had started again. Cheryl peered out the window at the threatening clouds that evening and turned to check the weather forecast on TV. She would be seriously behind if this kept up. She was in the process of warming a fragrant pot of vegetable soup. It felt right for this rainy, chilly evening. She reached for her cell phone and dialed Larkin's number.

"You wanna come over for dinner? I made soup and biscuits." She laughed at the enthusiastic response and heard the back door opening almost before she put the phone down.

"I was already on my way over. I swear I was gonna invite you out to dinner, but this is a much better idea. Ummm. Smells wonderful." He reached for the spoon and dipped out a large portion. He blew, trying to cool it, but then impatiently sipped at the broth.

Swear words floated around the kitchen as he hopped up and down and grabbed for a glass of water.

"You just couldn't wait. Ole instant gratification David. I remember you," she said as she helped him to an ice cube.

"I twied to waith, but it thmelled so gooth," he said around the washcloth he had wrapped around the ice cube. "I'th all your fauld. Ou thouldn't oth made it so good." He frowned at her.

"Oh sure. Shift the blame to someone else for your own actions. I remember that one too." She smiled as she teased him, but was halfway serious. David sharpened his gaze.

"You're still mad at me about that plant, sweetkins? I am

sorry. I said I was sorry and I tried." He walked toward her but she backed away.

"No, that's not it, David. Forget it. I've had a rough day and I'm tired."

"I know, Cher. I'm sorry you had to see that. You want to talk about it now?"

"Let's have some soup first. The biscuits are just about ready. Sit down, and I'll get us something to drink. You still okay with milk?"

He grinned and grabbed a chair. "You remember that, do you? I'm a growing boy. Love my milk."

She served steaming bowls of chunky vegetable soup stocked with left over pot roast. Hot biscuits were ready. She joined him at the table and then popped up almost immediately.

"Forgot the butter. You want jam with the biscuits too?" Knowing his answer, she sat a jar of homemade strawberry jam on the table and then collapsed into her chair.

"I'm almost too tired to eat," she said but sipped the rich broth spoonful by spoonful. Delicious, if she said so herself.

"Your tongue too painful?" She watched David dig into the warm biscuits, as he slathered them with strawberry jam then licked his fingers. She squirmed and turned her head away.

"Nope. Just being cautious. Thought I'd give it a little more time to cool." He looked up and caught her eye.

She could feel her face turning red, and she glared at him wordlessly, as a grin left his entire face covered with delight at her predicament. Of course, it would. Plant killer and womanizer that he was. Women probably just dropped like flies in front of him. Didn't even need jam.

"Tell me about the murder," she said, trying to cool the atmosphere and guide it back to business. She spooned up some soup and gingerly handled a hot buttered biscuit as she waited for the story.

"I've actually told you about all I can. You knew we were looking for this man. He was from out of town, and we think he was supposed to meet with Sam Toledo. We don't know who killed him, but suspect it wasn't Sam. The two of them had a sort of business deal coming down, and we hoped to intercept it. There's one more man, the other one in the photo, we'd like to get our hands on. If he turns up dead, we might have something bigger than we expected in the works." He juggled his biscuit and blew on it.

"Do you know why the dead man was left on the Malone's property? And are they involved? That would be sort of important for me to know before I sign any contract to work with them." She concentrated on her soup and refused to meet his eyes. Enough was enough.

"We don't have any idea why he was there. As to the Malones, my advice would be for you to drop any contact with them for the time being." He finished his soup with a final slurp, then patted his stomach and kissed his forefinger and thumb in a gesture of approval.

"But you're saying you don't have any real reason to suspect involvement at this time. What if the Malones know nothing about this business? I really don't want to lose this job."

"Jobs come and go," he said breezily. "Best to be safe, Cher." His attitude had her ire rising like a frog to a buzzing fly.

"I'm already involved with Toledo and with your approval. Are you saying it's too dangerous for me to be there?" She knew she had him.

He frowned and sat forward in his chair with a firm thump. "I hated it that I've had to ask for your help. I wish you'd just said you couldn't do it and canceled any contract."

"I have no intention of doing that. I did sign a contract and I won't just cancel without reason. All you have are suspicions. True?"

He ran his fingers through his hair in a parody of frustration which made her grin.

"Cher. Why can't you just do as you are told without all these questions? You are the most stubborn of little girls I've ever . . ." He hit his fist quietly on the table.

"Wait just a darn minute. Are you calling me a little girl? Look again, Larkin. I grew up a long time ago. And I make my own decisions. You aren't my father and I doubt if I'd do what even my father said without a very good reason."

He came around the table, pulling her up to stand beside him. "Do you see how much smaller you are than me?" He rested his head on hers momentarily. "You are a grown-up woman, but still little. Sweetest little girl. Been my favorite since you were thirteen." He swooped down and landed a fierce kiss on her up-turned lips, holding her to him by the back of her neck with his other hand around her waist. "I can certainly tell you are grown-up," he said, taking a deep breath, and she realized with horror that she had responded just as fiercely back.

Had she lost her mind? She jerked away and put a chair between them. Detective David Larkin, plant killer and seducer of young women who needed their heads examined.

"I'll consider your advice, David, but I must make my own business decisions."

"Then I will leave you tonight. If you have bad dreams, call me. I can be over in a flash," he said. He placed an arm around her as they walked toward the back door. "I really mean that, honey. I promise to behave. I don't want you scared." He molded her to his hard chest, his big arm wrapped almost completely around and laid his cheek against the top of her head for a moment. Then he tilted her face up to him staring deep into her eyes before abruptly letting her go and disappearing into the night. She stood motionless until she heard his back door slam shut, and then had to fight against the sudden vacuum his leaving had left.

So strange. Her feelings for this too-handsome-for-her-own-good man were in such conflict. She wanted him to leave and the minute he did, she wanted him back. She was sexually attracted to him and yet terrified of the depth of her feelings. She fought an ever-losing battle to maintain control over them. And longed to lose the battle every time she was within ten feet of him.

She trundled into an old and well-loved T-shirt that extolled the virtues of digging in the dirt and a pair of don't-ask-where-they-came-from boxer shorts. Waves of weariness swam over her muscles, and she crawled thankfully into bed. And lay there not sleeping. When her eyes closed, she could see grotesque bugs crawling out of the dead man's nose. *Eww.* She sat up in bed, turned on the light, grabbed a book, and attempted to read herself to sleep. Almost there. Finally, she turned out the light and closed her eyes.

What was that noise? She lay rigid, not moving a muscle while she strained to hear and identify the noise from the front room.

Probably the parrot. She could shift around in her cage and make all sorts of . . . No, that wasn't the bird. Cheryl reached quietly for her cell phone which was on the nightstand and just as quietly, hardly breathing, she dialed David. Better to be embarrassed because she panicked, spooked over finding . . .

"David?" she whispered.

"Cher, that you? What's up?" He sounded wide-awake, thank goodness.

"Someone is trying to get inside the office. Keeps rattling the doorknob and scratching around at the windows. Can you come over?" Her nerves were stretched to the limit, her breath caught on a sob.

"Hang on, sweets. I'll be right over. You stay in your bedroom so I don't trip over you in the dark, okay?"

She nodded as if he could see her, but he was gone already. She could hear dead air.

She lay with the covers pulled over her head, hearing what she wished she couldn't. Someone was determined to break into her shop and now rattling her bedroom window. She could hear the parrot, awake in her cage, squawking, "Naughty Boy." But she knew it wasn't David.

The window right beside her bed rattled and started to rise slowly. Terror shot into her veins and speed raced around her body. The night was full of horror, all looking like dead men with insects crawling out of every orifice. She jumped out of bed, ran for the bathroom, and locked the door. She opened the cupboard underneath the sink and tried to stuff herself in. Too tight . How to hide? She curled herself into a ball and huddled on the floor. Where was David?

Then she heard a man shouting outside. She opened the bathroom door cautiously and peered out. Loud shouts and cursing. David seemed to be trying to persuade someone to do something. Not even the dim light from a nearby streetlight could penetrate the darkness. She screamed as a distorted face pressed itself directly against the glass of the window.

David called out to her to open the back door. Was he kidding? She leaned against the door but screamed again when something large slammed against it.

"Cheryllll," someone called out to her, but the distortion in the voice . . . Who was it? He sounded vaguely familiar.

David called out to her again.

"I'm not opening this door to some monster," she called back. She heard David, her hero, the Monster Killer, laugh, but curse the next moment.

"Not a real monster, Cher. Just a drunk one," he said. "Open up, honey. Just long enough for me to get this . . . Will you stop it! I don't want to use force against you. Just calm down." He knocked on the door urgently.

Slowly, she opened the door with the night chain still

latched. She peeked through the opening to see David's eyes crinkled with laughter peering back at her.

"Open up, sweetheart. Nothing to worry about. Just one of your many suitors come to call. I think we need to infuse him with a bit of black coffee before we send him on his way." In he walked, dragging Gordon by the collar. A very, very drunk Gordon who smelled as if he might have vomited on himself. He grinned foolishly at Cheryl.

"Not a pretty sight," David said. "You might want to go back to bed and let me handle him, honey. He promised me he would behave if only he could see you for just a minute. Seen enough, fellow?" David winced as Gordon started weeping copiously and reaching for Cheryl. "Too much! Okay, let's go. Gordon, is it?"

"I'll call for a black-and-white to give him a ride home. He's really gone. No sense in sobering him up tonight. He can find his car tomorrow. It's not in the driveway. I wonder if he even remembers where he parked it." He dragged Gordon out the back door, turning to wink and blow a kiss to Cheryl.

Cheryl stood like a stone statue. *What more could happen this day?* Exhaustion ran in undulating rings around her body as she crept quietly back to her bed. She thought of Detective David Larkin, Superman, the ex-boyfriend handler, her friend, and sometimes plant killer who caused the ladies to lose their minds.

She thought about his grin and wink as he left her to drag the disgusting sot out into the night. *David is my hero. Superman with brown eyes and . . .* Sleep overcame her quickly.

Chapter 11

"How To Make New Friends and Share With Your Neighbor"
By Cheryl

Unlike a garden of annuals, which reaches its potential in one season, a perennial garden demands a bit of patience. The first year the plants set their roots and nothing much happens on top. This is when I suggest a supplement of a vivid crop of annuals. The second year is one of growth and beauty with the perennials coming fully into their own.

The third year has the gardener looking around for new places to put the perennial which now needs to be split. Its vigorous growth has exceeded its allotted space and . . .

"Doggone it. Who could be up this early?" Cheryl ran to the back door and peeked out. Larkin. Looking as bedraggled as she felt. She opened the door and was immediately enfolded in a bear hug, the male smells of pungent soap, spicy shampoo, and the familiar fragrance of his shaving lotion surrounding her all at once. She breathed once deeply before she tried to shift away from his enthusiastic embrace.

"I love having you next door, Cher. Say you like it too," he pleaded. "It reminds me of when we were younger. Do you have coffee? You do! I smell it. Okay, I smelled it across the lawn, I confess. I am in dire need of sustenance." He finally let her go after a swift kiss on her nose and bee-lined it to where he spotted steam rising from a newly brewed coffee pot.

Cheryl stood watching him with a half-smile. Who could get mad at Yogi Bear? Last night, Superman Super Cop, and this morning, an affectionate Yogi smelling food. She joined him at the coffee pot and shoved a plate of cookies toward him.

"No breakfast?"

"Not a thing in the house. I meant to go to the store but I forgot," he said, shoving cookies down his throat. "I was headed to the donut shop, but the fragrance of that coffee captured me. I hope I didn't wake you?"

"No. I had some work to do." Almost the truth. Although she had slept deeply, she awoke feeling as if some disaster were about to happen. It helped to get busy. Her column always needed work.

"Did your boyfriend call about the car? I gave the keys to the uniform who drove him home. Boy, was he ripped."

As David gave her an interested glance, she became aware that his curiosity was at fever pitch. Needing coffee, indeed. He needed information, she'd bet her last pair of leather gardening gloves.

"Gordon Moore is old news. Just having a hard time accepting that someone as ordinary as me could reject him."

"Gordon Moore? Isn't he the famous doctor? Got a weekly TV show, don't he? One of the uniforms recognized him. Said he was a ladies' favorite. Boyfriend of yours, was he?" David swallowed the last cookie on the plate, but she could tell he was serious about the question.

"I was engaged to him for a short period of time." She took the empty plate to the dishwasher. "I broke it off. He seems to be stuck in a time warp."

"It might take a little time, Cher. Sometimes it does." He ruffled her hair and smiled like a big brother.

"Time," she exploded in frustration. "How much time? It was over a year ago, and he's insisting I go on business trips with him."

It was Larkin's turn to frown. "A year ago? Wow. He really does have it bad. Want me to have a little talk with him?"

"No. No. No. David, I can handle my own affairs. Please don't interfere. I do thank you for dealing with that fiasco last night, but it was only Gordon. I was still on edge from the afternoon horror and couldn't think straight. I overreacted. He's just a nuisance. Promise me?"

"Okay, okay. Unless you ask. You off to the Toledo's to work today? I see it finally stopped raining." He adjusted his loose jacket around his shoulder holster.

Cheryl was beginning to get used to seeing the butt of a gun peeking out from his jacket. He was David, alternately her hero or her nemeses, and she seemed to be helplessly entangled in his web. She determined anew to resist the magnetic pull. She'd never be an adult in his eyes if she kept allowing him to rescue her.

"See you out there, but don't look for me. Just one man to keep a look out for. By the way, he was last known by the name of Tim Griever and he speaks with a slight accent. Again. Don't acknowledge him. Just call on that phone they gave you. Okay?"

She nodded, wondering if David thought she was a complete moron.

"I get a kick out of seeing my little girl bossing those great big equipment workers around. Not bad, Cher, sweets, not bad." He swiftly exited, leaving Cheryl speechless.

Its vigorous growth has exceeded the allotted space and is threatening to overtake more precious perennials. Your neighbor who has always admired your garden is probably drooling over your plants. Offer her a chunk of the perennial, keeping in mind to scoop deep enough to get plenty of healthy roots. Give her a few tips on the plants habits, such as 'needs a bit of space.'

Still got at least three splits to go? Make an announcement at coffee hour at church. Or go up to that shy lady and tell her you have an abundance of a very pretty perennial. Believe me, it works. New family in the neighborhood? What a nice house warming present! Try it.

Finally the rain stopped and the work could resume. Although they were a couple of days behind, Cheryl was confident they would still meet the deadline. The subcontractors were probably already on the job. She had an appointment with Francine regarding perennials. Should have done that in the shop, but Francine swore she couldn't leave the house today. No matter. Her flip-card brochure was pretty old-fashioned compared to her spiffy program with a nice big monitor.

Cheryl decided not to think about Sam Toledo and his criminal activities whatever they were, nor dead bodies left underneath oak trees. Her only assignment was to recognize a specific person if he came to visit. That was it. It was neither to think about solving the crime nor to think about who had killed that man.

The Malones were another problem, but it was work she couldn't really afford to turn down. If information got out that she refused to take a job as big as this one, it would damage her reputation. Ugh! She tried to push the image of the dead man from her thoughts. She joined her subcontractor and busied herself in work.

The recent rains had tumbled a few shrubs, but on the whole, the new plantings had stayed in place. The gentle slope to the terrain helped the drainage, so no puddles or mud formed. The sun was rapidly drying the grounds, and it promised to be a perfect day to work outside. She inspected everything with a critical eye.

The intimate little patio was a success and made her feel good inside. Surely it was acceptable to feel pride in a good job done? It looked as if it had been there for years. Getting away from the job for a couple of days gave her a different perspective.

Francine, dressed in a robe of pink silk, was waving a tissue in her hand. Her much bleached hair was hanging down her back, but her rings were flashing.

"Yoo-hoo, Cheryl. I have coffee and a coffee cake. I really like cake even if it's bad for my figure." She smoothed the robe outlining her bosoms and hipline clearly. Cheryl imagined the scene was catching the eye of a few of the contractor's workers and wondered where Larkin was, but she kept her promise not to look for him.

She followed Francine into the house and into the kitchen. Cheryl pulled her brochure from her over the shoulder bag and opened it to the first page of flowers.

"Oh, let's chat for a bit, shall we?" Francine waved her hand. "I need woman talk before I get down to business, don't you? This rain has had me cooped up for days and days."

Cheryl agreed that she preferred sunshiny days as well. They munched the sweet pastry and sipped coffee. Cheryl relaxed when there was no sight of Sam Toledo. She really didn't mind Francine as long as she seemed interested in gardening.

"Oh, here is my sweetest baby in the whole wide world. Come to Mama, honey."

Cheryl tensed, expecting Toledo. Instead, Francine swooped up her tiny dog, nuzzling him on his head. The minute creature shook with palsy, his eyes budged alarmingly. Large sparkling rhinestones circled his neck, almost too heavy for such a small dog.

"Isn't he the sweetest doggie in the world, my little Pooky?" Francine demanded, holding him out for Cheryl to admire.

Cheryl patted him gingerly on the head, but the puppy snarled. She jerked back while Francine trilled a burst of laughter.

"He is a naughty boy. Aren't you, my sweet baby?" she cooed in his ear holding him close to her face. Pooky subsided, then curled his lip showing his teeth at Cheryl and gave a high-pitched bark.

Francine got up to feed the dog. "There. I have him busy for a bit." She took a chair again at the table. "You want to do that work now?" She settled her cupped hands underneath her chin with an air of expectation. Her blond hair flopped over her shoulders, but her face was completely made up with massacred eyelashes and blood-red lipstick. She pointed her rings at Cheryl.

"This is a new one Sam just gave me. Isn't he the sweetest thing?"

Cheryl nodded in agreement.

"Here are a few samples of the plants I recommend. Keep in mind we're arranging for most of these plants to be viewed either from the intimate patio or from the larger one in back of the house. The rule of thumb is for bright blooms—yellows, red, oranges— to be arranged further away and for the cool colors—pink, purple, blue—to be planted closer."

"Ohhh, I love this one. It looks perfect for my vases." Francine pointed to blue salvia with short stems, and Cheryl covered her dismay with a hasty flip of the brochure.

"Francine, I have big plans to have a cutting garden. But we'll wait on that. These are permanent plantings just for the landscape." She winced at the petulant frown on Francine's face.

"You could cut this type of flower, but the stems grow so short it wouldn't . . ." She heard a step behind her, and Toledo came in dressed in a flowing blue and gold robe.

He clapped a hand on Cheryl's shoulder and greeted her heartily. "You girls having a good time with the posies?"

Francine popped out of her chair and reached around the man who was an inch or two shorter than she.

"How did you sleep, lover?" she asked, kissing him on the cheek and clasping her arms around his neck. "You need a cup of coffee, my honey bun?" She stepped to the kitchen door and screamed, "Lizzyyy!"

Cheryl jumped nervously at the sudden noise, but relaxed when a maid in uniform appeared and began serving Sam breakfast. Francine continued to ignore her and croon gooey words to Sam, who was eating. Eventually he pushed his plate back, and Lizzy quickly removed it.

"Been noticing the work outside, Cheryl. You have those boys humping out there in spite of the rain. I told Franny here I was impressed such a little thing like you could order those big boys around." He laughed loudly and boisterously. "How long you think it's gonna be before you finish up?" He propped his arms on the table, eyeing her seriously.

"I should be finished by your deadline. We're at the point now where some rain won't slow us down. Most of the big terrain movements are over and the large trees are in the ground. It's just perennial and a few shrub plantings now. Francine and I . . ."

"You let my little girl pick out whatever she likes, you hear?" He patted Francine on the arm and slyly reached down and pinched her on the hip.

She jumped, frowned, but quickly covered it up with a sexy smile. "You are a devil, you are," she said, leaning over to kiss him.

He laughed heartily and patted her on the arm.

"Now about money. Might as well give you another payment. Any new expenses we didn't expect?" he asked. "Francine, get me that wooden box in the bedroom." She disappeared from the room.

Cheryl tensed at being alone with the man but gathered her courage. "Nope. Actually, we came in under budget, Mr. Toledo. I always ask a bit more than I think it will take so no one is surprised." She named a figure as Francine came back carrying a wooden box.

"Nice job. Now I have one favor to ask of you, Cheryl. You know we're throwing a big bash at the end of the week. Francine, here, and I would like you to be our guest, wouldn't we, Franny?"

Cheryl blanked out, speechless.

"Get yourself a swanky party dress." He opened the box and took out stacks of bills, handing them over. "Buy the best. That's me. Sam Toledo. Always buying the best." He laughed his boisterous laugh, barking until he choked. "Think that'll cover it?" He threw another stack of bills on the pile then closed the box with a snap.

Francine, standing behind Toledo, was staring at Cheryl with narrowed eyes, obviously not pleased to have Cheryl included in Sam's generosity.

"Er, Mr. Toledo? I really prefer to buy my own clothes, but thank you for your very generous offer. This will cover the cost of the garden renovation very nicely, thanks." She returned a couple of the piles of bills to him.

He pushed them back to her. "Nonsense. Won't have it. You buy a pretty dress and come to the party. I gotta go. You girls have fun now." He left the kitchen barking out orders for Lizzy to bring him his new suit.

"My baby is a very generous man," Francine said with a smirk. "You'd best just do what he says. It's much easier. Ask me. I know." She stood up with her coffee cup signaling an end to their interview.

Cheryl felt numb. What had she gotten herself into now? No way was she going to be guest of a criminal and his gun moll. She closed her brochure deciding that Francine wasn't all that interested in choosing the plants after all. She could finish the selections by herself and, no doubt, no one would care.

"I'd better get back out there to supervise the contractor, Francine. Thank you for the coffee. I think I have enough information to finish the job now." She started toward the door.

"You know what I like by now, don't you, hon? I've got to get busy with my man. He takes a lot of my attention, and I don't intend to let him miss me too much." She smirked and abruptly left the room.

Cheryl felt as if her head was spinning around like a top. David had warned her not to interact with these kinds of people and she wouldn't listen. Oh, but then he wanted her to interact and spy. He was an irritating man. She hoped they would catch the thief or murderer or whatever they're looking for. She wondered if the second man was the one that killed the other. Her imagination formed a visual of the two men dueling it out underneath the oak tree.

"No," she said as she walked down the slope to where the contractor was planting a flowering shrub in its prepared resting place. "I refuse to entangle myself anymore." She raised her hand in greeting. The owner of the landscape company she had called to move the largest plants operated his own heavy equipment. Tom Hager was just starting out in business, and they each referred to the other whenever possible.

"Hello, Tom. Can you believe how fast this job has progressed? The rain didn't slow you down too much, did it?" She walked over to the shrub and knelt to give it a final cover. "You gave this hole plenty of water in advance, right?" She knew Tom could plant a shrub. Why did she always need to second-guess?

"This slope is perfect for shedding the rain, but we ran water in that hole for a good forty minutes. Enough?"

"Of course. I'm sorry. I never intended to grow up to be a neurotic."

They laughed, easy with one another. She admired Tom and totally understood his passion for plants. They had formed, not a partnership, but a friendship. Tom was as reliable as the sun rising in the east.

The landscaper who dealt with the heavy stuff was a foot taller than she, but he had never 'talked down' to her. He respected her expertise in garden design, admired it even. He was a ruggedly handsome man in his mid-thirties with a deeply tanned face burned leathery. They had gone out together for a bite to eat, but Cheryl felt only friendly warmth toward him. However Tom felt, he had never once stepped over the line from friend to potential date. Why she couldn't she fall for him? No doubt her life would be so much smoother.

She glanced around wondering where Larkin or his men had planted themselves. Nothing looked out of order. Men were working, mostly planting grass sod to cover the bare places. They all wore hard hats on the job and had their heads down while they worked. Larkin wasn't the only man with large shoulders and huge biceps. She gazed across the landscape. *That one could be him, or that one over there.*

Nerves skittered across her back as she thought of the almost ultimatum Toledo had delivered. She was not going to be forced to do something against her will. He had already paid her more than he owed. By the end of the week, the job would be finished.

Dumb, she wasn't. Unless that other man made an appearance before the end of the week, Detective Fowler would surely urge her to accept the invitation to the party. Larkin would be delighted, she guessed. Or not. He didn't seem all that enthusiastic for her to be working for Toledo even though he had agreed to the deal. Oh, it was all so confusing. Why was she involved in police work? Did she get a degree from the police academy? No, she did not.

Her enthusiasm for the job had ended when the corpse turned up underneath the tree over on the Malone's land. It linked this job with the potential next one. She would give her dad a call after dinner tonight. Perhaps he could shed some light on the background of the Malones before she needed to decide whether to bid on the job.

Tom Hager would appreciate the referral, and they could both use the work. He waved to her as he backed his equipment up. One more shrub to fill the space around the new little patio and that section would be complete.

She felt a thrill shoot through her. It was heady business to see something which grew from her imagination turn into real life, and she felt a justified pride. Her eyes roved over the undulating hillside where a combination of evergreen and flowering shrubs clustered here and there. A flowering crab nestled near a Bradford pear where banks of perennials were tucked against an ornamental stone wall, while a graveled path meandered through it all.

Near the intimate patio were brightly colored clumps of annuals. A birdbath already had a few customers sipping from last night's rainwater. She intended to place a large Tuscany blue jar adjacent to the table and fill it with a combination of colorful annuals and cascading vines.

She was still wavering about the cutting garden. The decision needed to be made soon. Francine would want her 'blue flowers.' No way could she produce that magic so she intended to buy a bouquet from a florist as an end of the job gift. Blue lisianthus would do it. Never would she imagine anyone turning down a large bouquet of flowers that resembled blue roses. Lisianthus was a particular favorite of hers.

With her head firmly buried in her plans for the garden, she walked straight into David Larkin who beckoned for her to follow him behind a newly planted tall shrub. She looked over her shoulder and then slid behind the dense foliage where David grabbed her and kissed her firmly on the lips. She was almost getting used to being manhandled by Superman, the killer of precious plants, who turned into an Italian Stallion at the drop of a trowel.

Chapter 12

"David Larkin! Have you ever thought you might use a cell phone to communicate with me?" Head spinning, Cheryl fought to regain her composure.

"Yeah, but this is so much more fun. Honest, Cher, I tried to quit but you're fast becoming a habit. I swear."

Spying the twinkle in his eyes, she interrupted his easy tirade of promises by holding up her hands in front of her. "No, don't. You know very well you'll break your promises. You always have and it appears you always will." She stepped back being careful not to pack the ground around the newly planted bridal veil Spirea.

"Whoa. That's a bit harsh. I'm just teasing you, honey. Are you seriously upset with me?" He turned a wounded face toward her.

Cheryl felt as if she'd kicked a puppy. Why, oh, why, couldn't she deal firmly with this man?

She frowned at him with narrowed eyes. "Okay, I'll behave. Fowler wants me to tell you to come into the office this afternoon. Do you have time? I can drive you there if you need me to."

He held her arm to keep her from stumbling backward. "Oops. Gottcha, sweets. This ground is pretty irregular although I'm really blown out of the park by the changes you've made around here. Just moved stuff around and shaped it all up."

"It's called the design, Larkin. It's what I do." She shrugged, feeling her words were wasted on hardheaded

David Larkin—sexy but oblivious, part Superman, part dense German.

"I know, honey buns. And you do it very well, too. Who knew all those gardens you built in the sandbox would turn out like this?" He chuckled as she felt her face turning pink.

"I know a few things about you, too, Mr. Larkin," she said, and mentally added, *Mr. Plant Killer and destroyer of sand castles.* "Why don't we call a truce before I trot them out for the entire world to see? Perhaps your fellow officers would . . ."

"Okay, okay. Truce! I'm gonna get back to work. That friend of yours is a slave driver. You been out with him many times, have you?" he asked, almost too casually.

Cheryl wasn't fooled.

"Tom Hager? He and I are old friends. We share a lot of interests and yes, we go out to get a bite to eat now and then. Why do you ask?" She shot him a challenging spear with her eyes.

"No reason in particular. Just wanted to make sure he's not hanging around your house getting drunk." With that parting shot, he ducked behind the shrubbery and disappeared.

She should have known better. David was quick on his feet, often just pretending he was too dumb to figure out the score. She rubbed her lips where his kiss had landed. Perhaps if she got a steel rod implanted in her backbone . . . No, she wasn't certain she wanted to miss out on those casual and way-too-familiar kisses. Addictive, even when she pretended to dislike them. She'd never confess it.

Where would all this end? Detective David Larkin had moved next door and her life had been turned upside down. With rare self-honesty, she questioned, hadn't he turned her life upside down many years before? He hadn't been in her life for a while, but was never absent for long from her thoughts. She considered her crush on the man. She'd even gotten herself engaged, for heaven's sake.

Paid for and almost completed, the design was a success. She would have dinner with Tom when it was signed off to deliver his cut in the pay as well. He had his own crew to reward, Larkin included in that group. Before it was all over, David would probably be posing for a working man's calendar with shirt off and biceps bulging.

Detective David Larkin, Mr. July.

A shiver ran across her shoulders which Cheryl blamed on the slight puff of moisture-laden wind. She resolutely went back to work.

"I don't intend to go to any criminal gathering. And I certainly do not plan to buy a dress with his money!" Cheryl was sitting in the office of Detective Kevin Fowler. She was relating the conversation she'd had earlier with Sam Toledo. "He made it almost a threat for me to be there. I firmly expect to be finished with Mr. Toledo by the time his guests arrive. I agreed to be on the lookout for those two men but nothing has happened." She sipped from a very bad cup of coffee.

"I know how you must feel, Miss Esterbrook. And I do appreciate your patience. Especially in light of what happened over at the Malones. I'm sure you are very uncomfortable after that incident. We believe this group has some sort of internal issues which they've settled in their unorthodox manner. But we . . ."

"I can't believe you'd even ask me to be over at the Toledo place after all that's happened." She sat the cup down with a jerk.

"I understand your feelings. If we thought you were in any danger, believe me we wouldn't ask this of you." He leaned forward with his hands clasped in front of him.

"How can you be sure I'm safe?" She thought of how David kept popping up unexpectedly while she was working.

"We have men stationed all around you, miss. Only we can't enter the residence without exposing their cover. That's where we need your help. If you would only be patient for a few more days. Until the end of the week."

"I suppose you want me to continue spying at the darn party." She slumped in her chair, dejected, already guessing the answer.

"Yes," he said quietly. "If you would. You're in a unique position to observe first hand that which we can only see from the outside. You still have the phone I gave you?"

She nodded.

"We're still trying to get a couple of men inside with you, but, as yet, you're our best bet. Believe me, Miss Esterbrook, this is important work. I can't go into details, but I can assure you, these men are a blight on society. We need to rid our town of them," he added firmly.

"Okay, I'll hang in there until the end of the week. Under protest, you understand. If I get shot or something awful, I'm personally going to be upset with you all."

"If I thought that were a possibility, but I don't. You'll be fine," he finished then stood up, signaling an end to the interview.

David met her as she entered the hall. With his arm around her waist, he escorted her out of the building and opened her car door. Leaning in, he brushed her hair from her face, kissed a fingertip, and planted it on top her nose.

She stared up at him, losing herself momentarily in the warm, brown pools of his eyes.

"Can I take you out for dinner tonight?" he asked. "I know this great little restaurant."

She shook her head no, and his face fell slightly with disappointment.

"I have plans for this evening," she said, "but thanks for the invitation."

He slowly closed her door and backed away resting his hand on the open window.

"Not expecting the gardening man over, are you?" He studied the tip of his shoes then looked quickly up at her. It annoyed her that he was prying. Couldn't she ever be allowed to grow up? She didn't need a baby sitter. It wasn't funny anymore.

"No, I'm not expecting anyone over. I'm going out." With that, she drove quickly away, leaving him standing in the street staring after her.

As she drove home, she contemplated David Larkin in contrast to Gordon Moore and decided they were both annoying as hell. Gordon wanted not just a fiancée but also a shadow, a slave, a female at his every beck and call. No matter how she calmly explained to him that her work was as important to her as his was to him, he paid no mind. To him, she was her father's daughter and needed no salaried work. He was sincerely baffled that she would work with her hands—in the dirt! In that respect he was in agreement with her parents who were almost as confused.

True, they had paid for two degrees without a murmur of protest, the last one preparing her for the work she was engaged in at present. Her father was indulgent saying she should try out different jobs before she settled in for good. It was obvious he thought she would soon leave her venture on her own in Landscape Design. Her mother remained puzzled and disappointed in Cheryl's career choice. She was even more bewildered when Cheryl announced she had terminated her engagement to Gordon Moore. Her father only commented she must know her own mind, but Cheryl suspected he was disappointed as well.

She laughed, thinking of the night he'd come in for a massage and fallen asleep in her bed. He hadn't given it a second thought, falling into an old pattern of behavior from when they were kids. And she had protested only feebly. He was driving her distracted. She found it more and more difficult to resist him and resist she must or suffer a broken heart. The difference between Gordon and David was that with the former she had to resist him. On the matter of David, she had to resist herself. He was no more ready to settle down with one woman than she was likely to give up designing gardens. She drove into her own driveway with a sigh of relief. It had been a long day and she was feeling stressed.

"Mom?" Cheryl dropped down on the back steps and spoke into her cell phone. The reception seemed best there in the open air. The late afternoon fragrances from her garden drifted past her nose and soothed with its sweet scents. The little faux hummer moth skimmed past her face with his melodic humming sound.

"Is Dad home? He promised to check into the background of the Malones for me. May I speak with him?" Cheryl kicked off her shoes and wriggled her toes in the cool grass.

"Just a sec."

A few minutes later, her father came on the line.

"Dad? Thanks for your help. Did you find out anything newsworthy?" Cheryl listened intently and frowned.

"All on the up and up? Do you suppose they know nothing at all about the crime committed on their property then?"

"Well, that's a sort of relief. Just because we know nothing suspicious at this point doesn't let them off the hook. Can you keep your ears open for me? I must soon make a decision concerning their project. What do you think I should do? . . . I know I must make the final decision, but I did ask for your advice this time."

She smiled at her father's tactful answers. He really was trying very hard not to interfere in her life except as a support system. He was a sweetie, her dad.

"Okay," Cheryl said, "I know you'll support me and I appreciate you wanting to stand aside and let me make up my own mind." She sat upright and frowned. "Don't say that! You and Mom will be around for a long, long time." She made kiss, kiss noises into the phone and said good-bye.

What a thought. Gone from her life? It was the last thing she wanted to think about. She guessed no one ever did. All alone. That didn't feel very good at all. Her eyes drifted toward the hedge. Had it grown taller since she first came to visit? Almost she could envision a young boy with a wicked grin and coal black hair peeking through at her. Her pulse did a thump and she felt it race a bit. What would the world be like without David Larkin not in it for her? She abruptly stood up and entered her cottage.

She made a mental note to call Jane tonight. As she closed the door, the phone rang. Jane.

"Yes, we're on for dinner tonight, but would you mind if we ate here? I'm bushed from work." Cheryl eyed the red light blinking on her answering machine.

"I don't have the paperwork we need for the collection yet, but we can map out the route. Okay, I'll see you in a bit. I may be in the shower. Come on in, the back door is open."

After she ended the call, Cheryl opened the door to the refrigerator and wondered just what she'd feed Jane and herself. Tuna fish casserole? Tuna salad sandwiches? That would do it. She had some fresh, vine-ripened tomatoes and fresh lettuce from the garden out back. There were raspberries over ice cream for dessert. A banquet fit for a princess. She eyed the blinking red light.

With dread and a premonition, she pushed the listen button. At first, all she heard was breathing. Then a long sigh. Then a click. She couldn't identify the sigh but decided it could be a telemarketer for all she knew. The next voice was familiar and reminded her to collect the material they needed for the toy collections. She and Janie were on that committee. The next caller was the breather again.

Why it bothered her she wasn't sure. Could it be the involvement she'd recently had with dead bodies and criminal types? Could it? Or being sort of threatened by a mobster boss if she didn't attend his party? She listened for more messages but that was the last.

She then headed for the shower trying to convince herself most of her worry was vivid imagination. Folks didn't always leave messages when no one answered. It wasn't David the Casual Kisser. He wouldn't have passed up the opportunity to grab her and plant a sexy one right on her mouth.

She stared at herself in the mirror and saw a pink blush paint her cheeks. *Okay, so I like those kisses. So what? I'm human.* Probably half the female police force liked his kisses. He was one sexy cop, killer of unique lilies, but sexy all the same. No doubt the Italian piece of the junkyard dog was the strongest. Or Superman. She wasn't sure.

She stepped into the shower and ran hot water over her hair. Letting her mind drift, she remembered her prom night. She'd been furious with David for spoiling her evening. Then he rocked her world with that long kiss which he deepened into a second one, groaning as he did. That sound made her feel powerful. Made her feel feminine, grown-up. If she could make big David Larkin groan, she must be desirable. Her feelings were totally confused for quite a while on the subject of David Larkin, next-door playmate who was too grown up to play with her anymore.

She scrubbed her hair, grinning and spitting water out of her mouth. He still wanted to play with her. He just couldn't get it through his huge self that she wasn't his little slave anymore.

She turned off the shower and reached for soap to lather her legs. Definitely time to shave. She heard knocking on the back door and stuck her head out of the shower and called out to Jane.

"Come on in, the door's open. I'm in the shower." She stepped back in the shower and turned the water on, shutting the opaque shower door. She saw a dark figure enter and sit down on the closed lid of the toilet.

"You'll get hot in here, Jane. I've been boiling myself under the hot water. It's still very steamy." She plunged her face back into the water for a final rinse and felt the coolness of the shower door as it slowly opened. Her heart thudded with the surge of adrenalin that raced through her veins. She screamed in surprise.

"Gordon! Get out of here! What are you doing? Are you crazy?" She yanked the door closed and turned the water off.

"Get out of here," she screamed. "Get out!" She could see him sit back down on the toilet.

"Don't get so upset, Cheryl. It's just a joke. You said for me to come in, you know."

It had been a long stressful day and she didn't need this kind of nonsense.

"Gordon, if you don't immediately exit this bathroom, when I do get out of here I'm going to have you arrested for breaking and entering. Or something of the sort. Get out!" She watched him slowly rise and open the door. He lingered at the doorway, and she screamed at him angrily. Finally, he closed the door. She jumped out of the shower, toweled off, then grabbed her robe, and used a hair dryer on her wet hair.

She knew she'd have to deal with the annoying Gordon so she might as well do it now. Jane would soon be over and she wanted him gone before then. She stormed into the kitchen where Gordon was sitting, sipping a cup of something. He acted as if he owned the place and it made Cheryl see even more red.

"Before you rip my head off, I apologize. That wasn't well done of me, but I couldn't resist. You did say for me to come in." Gordon grinned as he tried to coax her to better temper. She started to say that he knew very well he was not invited to her house, but he cut her off.

"I came over to apologize for my horrid behavior the other night. And to collect my car which is almost a block away. I hadn't had time to get a ride over here until now. Please say you'll forgive me?"

He took the fire from her anger with his apologies, but he didn't do a thing for her annoyance. What could she do or say to convince him the relationship was way over and done with?

Jane popped in the back door chatting about the balmy night. She stopped in surprise when she spotted Gordon.

"Oh. I didn't know you were a part of the toy collection, Gordon." She sat down at the table and the two of them started discussing the Christmas collections.

Cheryl wanted to pull her still-damp hair. She turned and walked out of the room to finish drying her hair and put on some clothes. Let the two of them sort it out. She'd about had it up to here! She pulled on a pair of sweatpants and a T-shirt, blew dry her hair, and pulled it back in a ponytail. *Voices in the kitchen? More than one male? Now what?*

She peered cautiously around the corner and saw David the Hedge Man making a fresh pot of coffee. *Now*, she asked herself, *how do you feel about his intrusion? Different? Oh, yes, you feel much different toward that sexy intruder with the hot kisses. What's he doing over here anyway, besides looking good enough to eat? Eat?*

How could she get rid of the two men? She was supposed to feed Jane tuna fish sandwiches. Could she claim measles? The plague? An infestation of ants?

Chapter 13

"Just put the annuals tightly together in that urn," Cher directed. "We want to place all of the containers where they will create strong splashes of color to fool the eye that the garden has been around for longer than a week or so. It's not the final solution, but my job was to make the yard ready for guests by this weekend. We have three days to finish. Think we'll make it?"

Tom Hager looked up from where he was popping colorful annuals from 4-inch pots. "Oh, sure. This is almost the end of the plantings. We still need to sod several places, but I wanted to wait for the ground to dry out more. Don't want to get the equipment mired in mud this close to finishing." He pushed hair out of his eyes with his forearm.

Cheryl admired his placid, good-natured face. Her own nerves had been stretched thin since her meeting with Detective Fowler earlier in the week. She had tried and partially succeeded in avoiding a meet with Sam Toledo, although his girlfriend, Francine, had been running in and out. She saw a caterer's truck arrive, stay for a couple of hours, then leave. She presumed Francine was picking out food the way she did colors for the garden, impulsively, indiscriminately, and expensively.

The dress for the party was still hanging over her head. Surely she had a cocktail dress in her closet so she wouldn't be forced to spend Toledo's money. That really rankled. Detective Fowler had advised her to go along with whatever Sam Toledo requested. Within limits, he qualified. Thank goodness for that. As far as she was concerned, the limits had already been breached.

She used her soiled sleeve to wipe her forehead. The sun was out and it was heating up. She was stuffing annual after colorful annual into one of the blue urns, deliberately over planting to compensate for lack of growing time. With the organic fertilizer she had seeded the potting soil with, they would soon explode and fall over the side of the container. Perhaps the hired full-time help would handle it. It wasn't in her job description. If she thought about how sad it would be for all her work to be neglected she would get upset. Detachment was the name of the game. Her work left her free to think, and she continued to plant while she mused.

Speaking of limits, she couldn't believe her house had been invaded not only by the annoying Gordon—again—but by David Gillard Larkin, Hedge Hopper, who had joined Jane and Gordon and was sitting comfortably at her kitchen table chatting, the three of them as cozy as kittens in a basket. She heard her friend giggle and stare adoringly over at Larkin, beast of the neighborhood, who was encouraging her friend, all the while pretending he didn't see her standing at the doorway. Gordon had his back to her and wasn't aware she had reentered the room, but she was well aware that David was faking ignorance. She knew him better than he thought she did. He had straightened, almost imperceptibly, but not quite, as she rounded the corner. He knew she was there.

She stalked into the kitchen without a word and made two tuna sandwiches. She ignored both men as she sat down at the table to have her dinner with Jane who finally got the point and quieted down.

"Looks like the two of us are out of luck, Gordon," David said, slapping him on the shoulder. "What say you we go down to the pizzeria and have a couple of beers and leave the ladies to themselves?"

His voice was casual, but Cheryl had looked up, noting the underlying steel in the suggestion, as apparently did Gordon. He rose with alacrity and both men left. David patted her on the shoulder as he passed by. She managed to ignore him, but was confused about her feelings.

Gordon was a pain but she really didn't need David to baby-sit her again, chasing off unwanted advances from unruly men as if she were still a green teenager.

On the other hand, well, she couldn't deny it gave her a nice feeling to have an advocate when it came to Gordon. He was getting to be more of a handful than she'd anticipated. It was obvious she needed to deal with him another way.

She turned to pay closer attention to her plantings. After putting the finishing touches on a picture perfect, color chart combination of twelve-inch golden marigolds and deep blue, cascading lobelia, Cheryl contemplated her options.

A restraining order seemed a bit harsh. Gordon was a professional man. Publicity like that would harm his practice, and she didn't want to go that far, but it had to end. It might be her imagination, but it appeared Gordon was growing more aggressive and making more attempts to control her, not less. He must think he would eventually wear her down, and she would resume the engagement.

"What a pain," she said, and then concentrated on the plantings. The work soothed her, and she found a rhythm that soon had most of the urns filled to capacity. She sat back on her feet, work boots digging into the soft soil, to wipe the sweat from her eyes.

Tom drifted over across the yard with his flats of petunias and was tucking them into the newly formed raised beds. He was using sweetly fragrant, white alyssum to form a border in front. Already, the colors were sparkling and the landscape was taking on a more mature façade. Not the famous/infamous blue petunias, but very nice anyway.

Which reminded her she had to set up a cutting garden for Francine by tomorrow. She turned when she heard a "yoo-hoo" calling to her from the house.

Lizzy, the maid, was gingerly making her way to the bottom garden where Cheryl was working. The young woman was holding her apron up to her chin as if she thought it would get mired by the remaining mud.

Cheryl stopped her work and waited.

"Miss Francine wants you to come to the house, please, miss." Lizzy squinted in the sun and smoothed her hair which was blowing in the slight wind.

Cheryl felt her heart sinking. The very last thing she wanted was to be inside with either of the inhabitants of that house. How to avoid it, she wondered, even as she started up the hill wiping her hands on her jeans. What the hell did they want with her now?

She looked around, hoping to spot David or some of the other detectives or undercover policemen. No such luck. Always around when she didn't want him and never when she did. She gritted her teeth and followed the maid into the back door foyer.

Her worst suspicions were confirmed when she spotted Sam Toledo sitting at the table in the kitchen eating what must be a very late breakfast or an early lunch. Francine hovered around him and glared at her as she walked in. As her star rose in Sam's eyes, it appeared it was rapidly setting in Francine's.

"There she is," Sam said, slapping his hand on the kitchen table. He reached over and pulled out a chair and patted the seat of it. "Come on over here, girlie, and join us." He laughed heartily as if he had said something funny or clever, half-chewed food clearly visible in his open mouth.

Cheryl forced a smile and took a seat in the chair. Francine flopped down next to Sam and glowered at her.

"You think I don't notice what you're doing out there, but I keep an eye on my money all the time." Sam laughed loudly again. "Looks like you know what you are doing. Looks a lot better. You sure know how to boss those big fellows." Again, the hearty laughter. "I like that in a woman."

Francine glared at Cheryl once more and left the room.

"Don't let her upset you, little lady. She gets knurly if I look with favor on another woman." He reached over and pinched her cheek.

Cheryl had to steel herself to keep from bolting. *Two more days*, she thought, *just two more days and I'm out of here.*

The police chief and two of his nosy detectives owed her big.

"Thank you, Mr. Toledo. I appreciate your compliments, but if I am to be finished by the weekend, I ought to be out there working. Was there something especially that you wanted to see me for?"

He leaned back with a slight disappointment on his ruddy face. "You got that pretty dress picked out yet?" He resumed eating, stuffing the large quantities of food into his mouth.

"Mr. Toledo, I'm not comfortable using someone else's money for clothes. But I will come to your party in a nice dress. Honest." She forced a smile of assurance, she hoped.

"Got some important people coming. I need pretty women around to make them comfortable. You know what I mean?" He lifted his fork and raised his eyebrows to stare at her. "Be extra money in it if you stick around."

Cheryl stood up to leave. "I understand, sir, and I will try to help Francine host your company. But I won't be able to stay very long. I run a business, as you are aware."

"Don't you worry about that. Plenty of business coming your way if I say so. Just keep your mind on what's going on this week end and you won't regret it." He leaned forward and pinched her on the arm laughing heartily again.

Rubbing her arm, Cheryl slipped out of the kitchen without another word. A bruise was already making an appearance.

Enough is enough. She stormed into the garden, all the peace from the day of planting gone. Tom looked up and waved to her, but she was too cross to answer. To top it off, she spotted Larkin, the Pretend Gardener, across the yard. She walked across to him, picked up a clump of sod, and threw it at his back. "You got me into this. Every time I get within ten feet of you, trouble comes knocking." He reached up and pulled her by the arm to hide behind another newly planted shrub.

"Cher, honey! They can see you from the house. You wanna blow our whole operation?" He put his arms around her and gently squeezed.

She could hear him sniffing her hair. "In the first place, this is not my operation. You tend to forget that. I am only into this as a favor to your boss. I plant gardens. I do not spend my time catching criminals. That is your gig. *Not* mine." She shrugged away from him.

Tom rounded the corner and stared at both of them.

"Am I missing something here?" he asked. "You know this fellow, Cheryl? Yes, of course you do. You wanna tell me what's going on?" He looked from Cheryl to David, his pleasant face wrinkled in puzzlement and alarm. "Are you bothering the boss?" he asked, looking at Larkin who shook his head no.

Cheryl nodded yes with a wicked side-glance at David.

"Aww, Cher. I'm sorry I had to ask you to do this. Honest, I am. I want you to know I was against it, but we really needed someone on the inside."

As he listened, the alarm on Tom's face grew and he stepped between Cheryl and David.

"You're fired, Larkin. Get your things and get out."

David turned toward him with surprise as if he'd only just noticed the landscaper.

Cheryl decided David deserved the mess he'd made for himself and stalked off leaving the detective to untangle his affairs as best he could. She turned back momentarily to speak to Tom.

"He's not a threat, Tom. Only a nuisance. I do think he owes you an explanation. I have work to do. We need to finish this job in two days. Think we can make it?"

Tom, still obviously upset, nodded yes, but kept his eyes on Larkin.

As she moved to the other side of the garden, Cheryl could hear the fake landscaper's voice as he tried to convince Tom not to fire him. Tom was a good man and deserved better treatment. If Larkin didn't fess up, she would enlighten the landscaper herself. She needed all the protection she could get.

Guns! Did Toledo have guns? The sudden thought terrified her. Of course he had a gun. Didn't she see him with one with her own eyes out at the old mansion? And someone had already been killed, never mind that he was a suspected criminal. He was still someone who had been shot.

She couldn't believe she was still involved with Toledo. Why didn't she just refuse to cooperate? She sank to her knees beside the flat of marigolds. The pungent fragrance of the plants soothed her, and she resumed her planting, pausing to admire how the blue of the urn was accented by the gold of the marigolds. She'd used a reoccurring theme of gold and blue throughout the garden. Her thoughts drifted as they would when she relaxed with her work. Thank goodness for marigolds. For fast color they couldn't be beat. They would liven up the new plantings and hold their own all summer well into fall. She was a firm admirer of the marigold in all its forms. These were only twelve inches high, but their heads were fully four inches across.

The afternoon passed by quickly and she rubbed her tired shoulders, straightening and stretching. Tom and Larkin both had disappeared. She wondered if David had talked Tom out of firing him, but it was not her problem. She had enough on her plate. She gathered her tools and headed for the driveway where she had left her car. She saw Francine standing at the window, but she didn't return the wave Cheryl gave her.

On the way home, Cheryl stopped at the corner minimart and picked up a rotisserie chicken. Too tired to cook, she knew this would last her a couple of days. She pulled into her driveway with a sigh of relief. Never had a job been as stressful as this one had turned out to be.

Cher grinned when Ganymede squawked a greeting as she opened the blinds and flipped the open sign in the window. Who knew? Perhaps another paying client would drift in her door.

Cheryl took the parrot on her arm and entered the kitchen, where she kept a perch as well, although it was her personal preference not to interact with the bird. But she had promised her grandmother to look after the parrot. Gany tilted her head sideways to inspect the food package on the table.

"Sorry, Gany. But it wasn't parrot. You're probably a bit sensitive about birds in general, I guess." She washed her hands and put the teakettle on to boil, then prepared a plate with leaves of lettuce and a sliced tomato. Pulling a leg off of the chicken, she sat down in the kitchen chair with a tired thump and started eating. Her head was drooping, and she thought longingly of her bed.

She washed and put her dishes away hoping the tea would revive her to work on the proposed putting green. Even if she hadn't decided to take the job, still the task intrigued her. She took out a sketchpad and was soon moving trees and shrubs around on paper. Her eyes began to droop, and she rested her head on her arms for just a second.

"Awk! Naughty Boy!"

Cheryl awoke with alarm and looked around for David. She could see no one and turned to the parrot with a frown.

"Are you sending a false alarm, old girl?" She watched as the bird paced back and forth on her perch uneasily.

"There's no one here, Ganymede. You probably had a dream just like I did." She took the parrot on her arm once more and headed to the front room where she tucked the bird in and pulled the cover over the cage.

What had upset the parrot? Gany was pretty placid. Sometimes clients would cause her to squawk, but most of the time she just clacked her beak and murmured bird talk. David was bound to upset her, and she had been riled more lately as he popped in and out.

Perhaps the bird had heard David drive in next door. Cheryl peered out the window at the hedge that separated the two properties. Nothing. All dark. How had it gotten so late? She must have napped longer than she thought.

She began the process of putting her home to bed, including herself. A welcome shower, a short nightie, brushing teeth and scrubbing nails. She performed the rituals almost mindlessly as fatigue crawled over her shoulders in waves. Thankfully, she turned the covers back and crawled in. Instantly, she was asleep.

The rattle of the window beside her bed was faint and did not disturb her slumber.

Chapter 14

Two more days. Cher crossed her fingers they would pass quickly as she pulled on her work jeans and boots, preparing to labor in the Toledo's newly created gardens. Time to get a cutting garden started. First, she'd visit a couple of her favorite nurseries. This project would not be easy.

In July, the middle of summer, it would be almost impossible to plant a cutting garden ready for harvest. Francine would insist, of course, that she be allowed to gather flowers from her very own garden.

Cheryl opened the back door and viewed her lush backyard gardens. *I wonder . . . Might work.*

She eyed three containers filled with flowering annuals: lisianthus, zinnias, cosmos, giant marigolds, crocosmias, flashing their elegant, red-blossomed stems. She'd need to fight with the hummers for that one. If she could manage to transfer at least some of these, it might satisfy Francine.

The nurseries might have more she could use for supplements. There were plenty of Asiatic lilies and a few Orientals just beginning to show color. Easy to transplant them. Okay, she'd need to stake practically everything and hope a heavy rain would not wash the plants with no anchoring roots away, but it might work. Hopefully Francine wouldn't guess this wasn't the usual order of things.

She'd already decided to buy several large bouquets of blue lisianthus to present to Francine the day of the party, tomorrow, in fact. Hopefully the blue petunias Fran had admired would be long forgotten after she glimpsed gorgeous lisianthus, the most beautiful cut flower in the business. And all in blue to match the sofa, of course.

"That's a pretty face." Larkin slid his large body through the opening in the hedge holding two cups of coffee. "You wanna try my special blend, Cher?" He walked across the lawn gingerly and passed her one of the cups.

She beckoned toward the garden bench, and they both sat and rested their cups and elbows on the table. The early morning sun warmed their backs. They sat silent sipping the warm brew, watching the flicker of butterflies work the garden. A robin landed in front and tugged in the grass then flew away with a section of dried grass in its beak. *She's building a second nest of the season.* Her arm and David's nudged one another occasionally as they drank the dark, rich brew. All her annoyance at her neighbor had melted away during the night.

"Whatcha doing to that hedge, honey? I swear I didn't break it down like that." He was gazing at the shrubbery underneath her window.

Cheryl turned idly toward where he pointed and stared. Fear shot through her, and she grabbed David's arm, spilling his coffee.

"I didn't do anything," she said. "Are you sure you didn't break my shrubbery the other night when you were banging on my window?" She stood and went over for a closer look.

"Nope. I knew you'd have my head if I broke any more of your plants. I was very careful that night." He trailed behind her still holding his coffee. As he grew closer, his attitude changed, his expression already materializing into a cop face.

"This neighborhood isn't what it used to be," he said quietly as he inspected the large footprints underneath her bedroom window.

A pretty boxwood shrub was mangled. Cheryl dropped down beside it and picked up broken pieces. No saving this one, she thought, trying not to imagine who would have done this. Did she believe David?

"You didn't have another headache, did you?" She stared him directly in the eye and watched a guilty expression flash across his face.

"I shouldn't have done that, honey. I just fell into our old childhood pattern that night. It felt so familiar and my memory kicked in automatically. You were great not to yell at me for falling asleep in your bed. Did I ever thank you?"

"I don't really remember if you did or not. I'm not angry at you for that. I truly understood the feeling. I guess we're both having a hard time letting go of our childhood behaviors. Or at least letting go of each other's." She looked directly into his eyes before she turned away.

"But, David, if you didn't do this, then who did?" She stood up and searched around the house, looking for more damage, but finding none. It was just underneath the window where she slept. The thought made her momentarily dizzy, and she sat back down on the outdoor garden bench.

David was already doing a systematic search of her entire yard. He was on the phone to someone barking orders. When he finished, he came over and put his arm around her, pulling her in close.

"Do you know of anyone who would be snooping around here at night?" he asked.

Cheryl thought of Sam Toledo and his criminal friends and buried her face into David's hard chest.

"Toledo was pushy and too interested in me yesterday. That's why I was so upset when I came back outside. You don't suppose he would come over here?"

David's arm tightened around her, but he said nothing.

"I suppose it could have been Gordon. He's been making a nuisance of himself lately, but it certainly isn't his style—unless he was drunk again. I think he would more likely have knocked on the door or called me on the phone."

"Well, it could have been some kid wanting a peek at the prettiest lady on the block. We shouldn't over react. You keep your shade down at night, don't you?"

Cheryl shrugged. "I will from now on. And put the lock on the window. Funny, but I've never been frightened to live alone until lately." She pulled away from David and gave him a look. Immediately he shifted her closer again.

"It's not my fault, honey. I promise you I'll get to the bottom of this. I never meant for you to become involved in the first place. I'm going to talk to the chief and Fowler today. This is almost over, but I'm not going to see you disturbed anymore."

"No, don't. Two more days and it's over. If the police can take these men out of commission, everyone will benefit. I can handle it. Are you going to be at the job today? Did you manage to convince Tom to let you stay?" She started to pull away again, but David kept her tucked firmly to his side. To tell the truth, she wasn't all that uncomfortable.

"Yeah. He's a pretty nice fellow. I can see why you like him. You date a lot?"

"Why do you ask? Did Grandma suggest you to keep an eye on me?"

"I'm used to keeping an eye on you, Cher. You're my girl, my grown-up girl now." He reached down and tilted her chin and gazed into her eyes.

She thought he might kiss her but he just stared. She felt herself getting warm as her eyes stayed locked with his. The intimacy was warming her into an embarrassing situation. She wriggled a bit in his embrace.

"Yep. I'm all grown up now and I must get my adult self to work. You coming right over?" she asked.

"In a few. I wanna check in with Kevin Fowler and see how he wants to conduct the operation this weekend. There's been no sign of any visitors?"

"Caterers only. No one else since I've been there. I wish his company would make an appearance soon so he'd stop paying me attention. Francine is mad enough as it is."

David grinned. "Well, I can see her point. You put her brassy self to shame."

"Oh, sure, me and my sexy clothes." She glanced down at her work clothes and scuffed boots.

David, the Italian Stallion Letch, grinned even broader. "You're seriously sexy no matter what you wear, honey. You've been tearing me apart since you turned thirteen. Had to stay away from you there awhile."

Cheryl's face dropped in astonishment.

"You didn't know? Well, our grandmothers did. I got called on the carpet more than once and told to stay away from little Jailbait Cheryl. You're all grown up now, so be advised." He laughed as she punched him lightly on the shoulder.

"I don't worry. You're way too busy courting every female within a radius of fifty miles. I don't like sharing so I think I'm safe." She walked across the yard and down the driveway to her car. A glance told her that David stood staring after her until she drove away.

"Jane? Listen. You wanna go to a party with me tomorrow? . . . Where I've been working. I won't know a soul 'cept for the owners of the house. Why do you think I'm trying to drag you there with me? But you might enjoy seeing the house and garden . . .

"Full cocktail regalia. Yeah, little black dress time . . . No, don't bother with a hairdresser. We aren't likely to see any of these people again. At least I hope not . . .

"I'm trying to finish it up today. I should be out of there before lunch. Will I be glad! . . . No, not the work. I'll tell you all about it soon. Okay? . . . Can I pick you up around four tomorrow? I saw the caterers, so there's bound to be good eats."

After a few more minutes, Cheryl hung up and returned to work. The cutting garden might be her best feat of improvising yet. She had to restrain herself from giggling at all the little stakes in a row holding the blooming gladiola heads upright. But she had gotten the job done. Finished. Completed in two weeks in time for a garden party or something like that.

She hated to do it, but she knew she needed to return to the house to say the job was finished.

She looked around and spotted Larkin and another worker she suspected was a fellow cop. Tom was directing them in placing the last bit of sod. How they would manage to be around tomorrow she had no idea, but it wasn't her place to worry about it. She trusted David and his police department to keep her safe and that's all that counted as far as she was concerned. She sneaked a peek through a leafy shrub at David's wide shoulders and rippling muscles. Certain he couldn't see her, she paused to enjoy and admire her sexy neighbor. No doubt about it, he was one gorgeous hunk of eye candy and she was only human after all.

She walked briskly up the hill and tapped on the back door.

Francine opened it, giving her a cool stare but invited her in. "Sam's in his study. I presume it's him you wanna see?"

With a stomach full of dread, Cheryl nodded and stepped down the hall after Francine.

"Hello, Mr. Toledo," Cheryl said. "I'm here to let you know I've finished right on time." She stayed close to the door giving Toledo a bland face. He looked up and grinned at her. *The old lecherous dog*, she thought. *Let me get out of here.* But she held her ground.

"You all ready for the party? Frannie, here, has been

working hard too. She's about got me broke ordering the food and such." He waved his hand negligently at his live-in.

Frannie flashed him a surgery smile and stuck out her hip toward him.

"You see any of our guests yet, Fran?" His face changed to one of menacing steel as he glared at his live-in.

Cheryl clenched her hands together to keep from running out the door. It reminded her that this was a hardened criminal who was under police surveillance. And might be a murderer. She needed to conclude their business.

"I will be here tomorrow afternoon around five o'clock, Mr. Toledo. Do you mind if I bring a girlfriend along? I'll hardly know a person here."

His face changed as his gaze turned back her way.

"Suit yourself. Yeah. The more dames here, the better. Ain't that right, Fran?" He bellowed a laugh as Fran tried to contain her annoyance. "Take this check as a bonus because you got the job done right on time. I appreciate when a person keeps her word."

He gave a sharp look over at Fran who shifted her feet and stared out the window.

Cheryl didn't have a clue what that was all about but was delighted it need not be her concern. She reached for the check, and he grabbed her by the wrist, pulling her close to his face.

"Don't disappoint me, little lady. I expect to see you here with a pretty dress on. You remember that?" He stared her in the eye, and then suddenly released her as his laugh bellowed out again.

Heart pounding, Cheryl turned and left the room with a measured tread. She refused to let him see how intimidated she really was. Fran trailed her toward the door, but she opened it and escaped without a backward glance.

Outside, she waved to Tom who was walking toward the

house. There was no sight of David or anyone else, so she presumed the last bit of sod had been transplanted.

"I have a bonus check."

They bumped fists and grinned at each other. Not a bad profit for two weeks work. "You wanna go for a cup of coffee to celebrate?" Tom threw his arm around Cheryl's shoulder, and they headed for the parking lot and their vehicles. If it weren't for that darn party tomorrow, she might feel more festive. Anyway, they both had made hefty profits and it was a signal for a celebration.

"You were brilliant, Cheryl. Can't believe how you pulled that mess together. I laughed at that cutting garden with the stakes."

They sipped their outrageously priced cups of gourmet coffee.

"Hard to explain, but I'd promised her that from the very beginning. She wanted to cut her own flowers for the party. What was I to do? She had no idea that I couldn't just magically produce a full-fledged cutting garden."

"What?"

Cheryl looked up to see Tom staring her with a curious glint in his eye.

"You're something else, Cheryl. I do appreciate the chance to work with you. It's been both fun and profitable.

"Yeah?" She smiled at him. "That sounds like a but coming up. You saying goodbye or something, friend?"

"Nope. I hope you call me the next time and the next after that. But I am saying goodbye in a way. I finally figured out during this job that there's no chance for me to date you. Yes, I know you had no idea I wanted to." He tucked his head in embarrassment. "But I promise, I was working up to it." He laughed at her shock.

"Don't be upset. I know if you don't, that your heart is already given. And I know who has it too." He finished in a rush then covered her hand with his, both of them sporting grimy fingernails.

"He's a good man, Cheryl. I got to know him while we were working. He cares about you a lot and worries about you a lot, too. I don't know why the two of you aren't a couple. But it doesn't take Einstein to see that you belong together."

"Tom." She squeezed his hand. Why, oh, why, couldn't she care as deeply about this nice man as she did for that rogue, David from the Hedge, David the Parrot Teaser, David the Plant Killer, David, who invaded her space, always assuming he was welcome? And wasn't he?

Chapter 15

Cheryl looked up from her kitchen table to see the grinning face of her neighbor. The piece wasn't due for a week, but she had a good start on her next gardening column. David was not unexpected and not exactly unwelcome. She was still a bit nervous after they had found the trampled shrubbery directly underneath her window.

"Cheryl, have you had dinner yet?" he called as he stood impatiently rattling the screen door.

She tried, and failed, to hide the grin on her face.

"What do you have in mind?" she called back without leaving her seat.

"I have an invite that includes you. It's a surprise, though. Can I come in?" he asked with that purring tone to his voice.

She stood and made her way to open the latch. Immediately, he opened the door and had her in his arms. She stood placidly for a minute breathing in the essence of David, her nemesis and her love. Yes, she loved him. What that meant for the future, she wasn't certain.

"Where are we going?" she asked, without moving away.

He caressed her back and rubbed his face in her hair. "Umm, sweet Cher." He tilted her face up with one finger and placed a light kiss directly on her lips. Unexpectedly, he moved her away and flopped down in the kitchen chair.

"It's a barbeque. Do you need to change clothes? You look pretty okay to me, but I know you've been working hard today. Can you be ready in about an hour? I'll come get you." He stood, kissed her on the forehead, and walked away, assuming her answer would be yes.

Cheryl laughed and headed for the shower. What use was it to make a fuss? With David Larkin she'd have to choose her battles and an outing sounded fun. She wondered who was hosting this outdoor party and should she be bringing a dish to pass. Oh well. She'd write a pretty note in thanks later for whoever it was. Although Hubbard had experienced a growth spurt in the last couple of years, she pretty well knew most families in the village.

The thought of a party cheered her considerably. It had been a big relief to finish her project at Toledo's, but she still had to make an appearance at the gangster's party the next night. She tried not to think of it. Whenever she thought of presenting herself to the exposure of those criminals, her stomach tightened in knots.

She dried her hair and chose a bright yellow peasant blouse to top a pair of white jeans. Sandals completed her outfit and she added a gold bracelet, a gift from her parents on her twenty-first birthday. She stood irresolute in front of her mirror wondering if . . . Yes, she selected tiny gold hoops for her ears. A quick application of lipstick, and she was good to go, just as she heard the rattle of the screen door and the sound of her name floating on the air. She hurried to join David, the party animal.

"Okay, where are we going?" she asked as they sped down the street in David's unmarked cop car. She knew he was exceeding the speed limit, but somehow she wasn't uneasy. It wasn't his size that made her feel safe, was it? No, it was something different. This was a grown-up David, a cop through and through. He was still her childhood friend, but he was many things more now, and she was starting to not only accept it, but to like it.

"You know the host and hostess, Kevin Fowler and Beverly Hampton. I think they are about to be married. I know for sure they are engaged. They like to entertain with cookouts. I have no idea who all else will be there, but Fowler said for me to bring you especially. I think he feels guilty for putting you in the situation you've been in lately."

"Oh," Cheryl said, surprised but pleased. "I know Beverly has been working on her landscaping in that older home she bought. I'm excited to get the chance to see it. Thanks." Cheryl grinned, and David gave her a quick sideways wink and patted her on the knee.

The heavy summer greenery on the trees drooped and formed a tunnel as they drove though the residential area of the village and found the side street. Cheryl loved the tidy front lawns and flowering hanging baskets favored by the residents. She noticed a resurgence of perennial gardens decorating the front yawns. A teardrop shape seemed to be the preferable design, but an exception was her favorite. A classic perennial garden backed up to an attractive, white-picket fence.

Large patio pots placed on the friendly porches displayed a variety of ideas. Some of the designs belonged to her from her gardening columns, and she couldn't help a surge of pride and felt a happy lift to her mood.

Traffic was quiet on the streets at the dinner hour. David found the driveway already crowded with guests and had to park halfway down the street. He took her hand as they walked down the sidewalk toward the gracious older home.

"You okay with this, Cher?" he asked as they approached the gracious porch where two rocking chairs sat, one occupied with a curled up and sleeping orange cat. An enormous patio pot of petunias overflowed on the middle steps.

"Very much so. Beverly is the editor for my gardening column, you know. We've known each other forever. I'm pleased you accepted the invitation for us both. Detective Fowler seems to be a nice person in spite of his insistence on my exposure to hardened criminals." She laughed to see

David shrug his shoulders and wince as he knocked lightly on the screen door. She could hear voices and music drifting throughout the home.

A man who looked like Detective Fowler, but a younger version, answered the door. "Welcome, Larkin. Who is this lovely you've brought us?" He opened the door wide to shake David's hand.

"Just you keep your eyes on that gorgeous blond. Brenda is about here somewhere, right? This is Cheryl Esterbrook, a childhood friend of mine. This is Kevin's baby brother, Ted Fowler, Cheryl."

He ushered them into the formal dining room where two couples were dancing cheek to cheek, as the music poured from a radio sitting on the table. They hailed David as he and Cheryl walked by and she assumed they were policemen. Finally they reached the kitchen, which was crowded with a mob chatting and laughing over a counter set up for liquid refreshments.

Declaring he intended to find them drinks, David left her to push through the group. She spied her hostess bending over the refrigerator and stood patiently waiting for her to emerge.

"Beverly, thank you for the invitation! Do I dare expect a tour of your garden tonight? Is it too dark to see?"

Beverly leaned toward her for a quick kiss on the cheek. "So pleased you could join us. There's a mixture of people here, but I think you'll find several that you know. I don't know what you will think of my amateur gardening. Please don't judge me. I'm still learning."

They made for the back door where Cheryl could see white smoke billowing from the large grill.

Several people were sprawled in outdoor chairs on an adjacent flagstone patio. A couple of teenaged boys were kicking a soccer ball back and forth in the deep backyard.

Kevin Fowler with an apron covering most of his tall, solid figure stood flipping burgers with flair. He turned as Beverly and Cheryl came out onto the patio.

"I see David Larkin still can persuade the ladies," he said with a grin. "I'm so pleased you can join us, Cheryl. David wasn't certain you felt we were a congenial group."

"What's going on, Kevin? Have you been treating my friend badly?" Beverly asked with a frown.

"Show me your garden, Bev, and I will tell you all about it."

They walked toward the side garden, a riot of blooming perennials.

"I just happened to be in a position to help the police department with some really bad people they had been investigating," Cher said. "It wasn't a pleasant thing, but it's almost over. I have promised to attend a cocktail party tomorrow night. All the police will be hidden and will watch over me."

"I'm sorry you had to do that. You are here with David Larkin, aren't you? I heard he has a thing for you. How do you feel about him?"

Cheryl felt her face go hot, and Beverly laughed.

"Never mind me. It's difficult to keep secrets with these fellows. They are natural snoops." She led the way to a garden bench placed strategically to the flowerbeds and offered Cheryl a seat.

"How do you handle his job?" Cheryl asked.

Beverly did not pretend she misunderstood. "It's scary sometimes, but he comes with the work. I couldn't give him up because I find his job uncomfortable at times, could I?"

Cheryl shook her head. She understood now that David was all cop.

"It's a brotherhood, Cheryl. Policemen and firemen have a solid brotherhood. They take care of their own. If you're around long, they'll adopt you too."

"I don't know the answer to that, if it was a question." Cheryl laughed. "No one has asked me to stick around yet." She changed the subject hurriedly. "I love your garden and the way you've incorporated the perennials with some flashy annuals. Are those crocosmias in the corner? Hummingbirds just swarm them. Remind me to tell you about the garden I just finished." She smiled. "It taxed my ingenuity to the limits."

All of a sudden, they were surrounded by a group pulling them forward.

"Kevin says to bring you to the patio. He has burgers and such ready." A tall, gorgeous blonde named Brenda was handholding Kevin's brother.

Cheryl recognized several other people she knew. They reentered the kitchen where David thrust a tall glass of something into her hand. He raised his eyebrows, and Cheryl understood he wanted to know if she was okay. She nodded and waved him away.

With her plate full, she found a place on the front porch with several other couples. Soon David appeared, sat on the floor with his full plate, and snuggled against her knee.

Cheryl acknowledged a deep feeling of contentment. Did she belong here with these people? Somehow it felt right.

David was smiling and joking with his colleagues, but kept his shoulder brushing against her as if he wanted reassurance of her presence.

Beverly came out, followed by Kevin, and together, they claimed the wide steps. Someone had usurped the rocker from the cat, but then was plagued by the loud meowing of a begging feline.

When Cheryl thought she could not eat another bite, a gorgeous brunette named Susan, who ought to be hired by someone to advertise hair products, came out carrying a huge platter of sliced cake and set it on the wicker table. There was an immediate scramble for napkins as they surrounded the table amidst slight shoving and bantering.

Cheryl found herself laughing until tears threatened at some of the quips. David grinned as he emerged triumphant with two pieces on napkins and presented her with one of his trophies.

Ted leaned over and teased her. "Any time you want to get rid of that hunk, just let me know. There's any number of better-looking gentlemen around here that will take his place. You just let me know."

She laughed even harder when she heard David, his face covered in crumbs, absolutely growl.

"He might be dangerous, but we can handle him, Cheryl."

It was another very handsome policeman whose name escaped her. She recognized him from the volleyball games.

He sat down near them and whispered directly to her. "Don't you worry, pretty lady. We're going to be right beside you tomorrow night. We don't intend for those bad guys to upset you one bit. Just look around you and you'll spot us close by."

"I appreciate it. I know you're on the job, but Toledo can be so obnoxious, I dread having to interact with him another time." She shook her head, and David shifted to catch her eyes. He stared at her with a serious face.

"You gonna be okay, sweet Cher? I'll be there close by, I promise," he said.

The other policeman nodded in agreement.

After another hour or so, Cheryl felt exhausted and tapped David on the shoulder. She needed to get some rest after her long day at work. They found their host and hostess to say goodnight, but it was a while until they could get out the door and leave.

"A congenial group of friends, David," she said as they wove their way back through the quiet village. It was only ten o'clock, but she could see many homes were dark already.

"Yeah, they're not bad people, I guess," he said with pretend casualness. "You enjoy the party?" He kept his attention on the road, but Cheryl could see the tension in his shoulders. He really wanted to know her answer.

"I very much did. I haven't seen Beverly in weeks. I email my column in to her, but we don't get to visit as much as we used to." It wasn't what he wanted to hear. She knew it, but some devilment kept her from sharing her feelings regarding all his policemen friends.

"Some of the fellows are a pretty rough bunch, but they don't mean you any harm, sweet Cher." He reached over to find her hand. "Did they upset you?"

"They seemed like a great group. I didn't know you were friends with so many firemen. I enjoyed chatting with their wives too."

"Yeah, we run into each other pretty regularly. Fowler is always up for a cookout. I was surprised when he and Miss Beverly got together, but they make a nice couple, don't they? She doesn't seem to mind being special to a cop." David gave her a sly glance with a half-smile.

If she didn't know better, she would guess David was a tad embarrassed. She had a lot to think about after this night, but she wasn't about to be rushed into making any kind of important statements. She changed the subject to the upcoming night.

Chapter 16

Limousine after limousine pulled up to the circular driveway discharging passengers. Jewels sparked on the women, and tuxedos wrapped around men who appeared stiff and uncomfortable. It must have been her imagination, but Cheryl thought she saw suspicious lumps in a couple of the men's coats. How many were carrying guns? She tried to control her imagination and remembered that David and his friends were . . . what did they call it? The police were packing heat too.

She and Jane walked together up the concrete drive while Cheryl pointing out features in the newly planted garden. She was carrying a double order of lisianthus, the Echo variety in deep blue. One of the favorites of florist since it stayed fresh in the vase for so long. Not to mention how it resembled a partially open rose in an unbelievable deep blue.

"Dunno what it looked like before, but it's beautiful now. You're so talented, Cheryl. I envy you." Jane walked over near the beginning of the garden and used her cell to take a quick snapshot.

"Stand over there, Cheryl," Jane directed. "Let me get the designer with the garden in the background."

Cheryl complied, thinking it might be useful for future jobs. She chuckled thinking a landscaper designer in a cocktail dress was hardly suitable advertisement.

"I enjoyed planning it," Cheryl said, "and even more watching my ideas develop, but I confess I'm really glad the job is over. Anyway, my friend, Tom, and his crew did most of the work. Are you ready to make our appearance?"

"Sure. Didn't you promise me lobster patties?"

They were laughing as they entered the house which was crowded with people, none that she recognized. She gave a sharp lookout for Tim Griever but hoped she wouldn't see him. Where were David and his buddies? They had to be here somewhere. An arm grabbed her around the waist and pulled her into a closet. Her pulse jumped and she stiffened with fear.

"David, cut that out! You scared me to death. Where's Jane?" She started laughing when she recognized the uniform of a plumber. No wonder he had managed to get inside. She immediately relaxed. "Are the rest of your team dressed the same? How many plumbing problems do you think you can pull off? Where is Jane?" she asked again.

"Shhhh. She seemed to be headed for the food table. Listen, honey, plans have changed. We've discovered that all the parties are present, and we're about to make several arrests. You need to get out of here. Think you can grab Jane and go out the back door? We tried to call you, but you had already left. You need to share your cell phone number with me first thing tomorrow. Promise?"

"Okay. I won't be sorry to leave, I assure you. David? Cut that out."

He was planting a kiss on her lips, which had her heated beyond what the stuffy closet was causing.

"Sorry, sweets. You smelled so good. I'll behave now. Grab Jane and slip out."

He opened the door, and they both exited, Cheryl to head for the kitchen, David to move toward the den with a plumber's toolkit in his hand. She smiled to see him in a coverall a size too tight for his wide shoulders.

Cheryl froze when she entered the kitchen and spotted Jane. A man was holding her with one arm wrapped around her waist. He also held a gun to her head. Jane's face was frozen in fear, but she rolled her eyes wildly when she realized Cheryl had entered the room. Was she trying to send a message?

"Just keep quiet, and you won't get hurt. Stand over there. No, over there." He motioned with his gun toward the corner.

Cheryl walked slowly by the two of them, staring at Jane, who continued to roll her eyes. Now Cheryl realized it was in terror. She wished she could reassure her friend, but she was paralyzed with fear herself. These were not nice people. Hadn't David told her that enough times? Why hadn't she listened to him? Why did she need to be so very stubborn, insisting she knew everything?

David rounded the corner and stopped short when he spied Jane and the man whose picture Cheryl had seen in Detective Kevin Fowler's office.

Griever motioned with his gun. "In the corner. Over there!"

David was still in disguise, and the man had no idea he was a policeman. He walked gingerly across the kitchen floor and nudged Cheryl, who was struggling with the fear which threatened to overwhelm her.

Francine entered the room and uttered a short scream when she spied the grouping in the kitchen.

Griever called her name.

"Francine! Honey. I'm sorry. Come over here, please." Francine stood frozen in the doorway.

"What's going on?" Sam Toledo stood behind Francine thrusting his head around her shoulders. He pushed her aside with a grim frown on his face.

"Griever, I told you to get lost. Now get out of here. You and Geer messed up. You don't get back in after that. Understand? Now leave before I hafta get rough." He ignored the gun which was still pointed solidly against Jane's shaking head.

Cheryl felt David edging toward Jane and the man with the gun.

Suddenly, a tall man appeared behind Toledo, grabbed his arms, and handcuffed him. David simultaneously slammed his hand against Griever's arm and pulled Jane away. He wrestled with the man over the gun which discharged into the floor. He reached underneath his shirt and pulled out a pair of handcuffs. After he was restrained, Griever collapsed against the kitchen counter. Another plainclothesman entered and dragged him out the door. Cheryl took a deep breath and held out her hands to Jane.

David wrapped both her and Jane tightly in his arms. Cheryl knew she was shaking and could see how upset Jane was as well.

"So sorry, girls. We didn't expect that. Let me get you out of here." He hustled them out the back door. "Do you think you can get home now? I'll be over later to see you, okay?"

They both nodded yes, and he hurried back inside.

A black-and-white pulled up, and Malcolm, David's friend from the police force, exited the car. He waved and beckoned to Jane, who turned back to stare at Cheryl.

Cheryl smiled shakily at her friend, who nodded and then joined the policeman at his cruiser. She entered the car with the Malcolm. As the car pulled close, Jane leaned out.

"David is going to be with you shortly, right? Malcolm is going to take me home and sit with me for a while if it's okay with you. Will you be all right, Cheryl?"

She assured them she would be fine and gazed after them as they drove off. What about that? Malcolm seemed like a really nice fellow, and Jane deserved a nice man after the rotten one she'd just dumped. She hoped Malcolm intended to stay with Jane for a while, perhaps even spend the night. Jane had had the worst of it. How long did it take to recover from having a gun pointing at your head? Cheryl felt guilty for dragging her friend into the danger.

After she finally arrived home, Cheryl pulled the cocktail dress off and slid into a pair of sweatpants and an old sweatshirt. She intended to make herself a cold glass of tea and sit in her garden and do absolutely nothing. She needed to regroup after that excitement.

The sun was starting to set with the day turning into velvet twilight with moths, hummers, and butterflies still working the garden. Bumblebees buzzed by loaded with yellow pollen. She could hear the soft, mournful call of a dove somewhere close by.

Even though her time with the Toledo crowd was over, Cheryl still felt shaky. She padded barefoot out into the cool evening. The grass felt marvelous to her toes. She sat on the stone bench remembering an evening when she had been there with David as scenes of the two of them interacting flashed through her mind.

What if he moved away? Sold his grandma's house? She didn't think she could survive the loneliness. Protest all she liked, but she had come to rely on his company. It was comforting just to know he was close by and would come if she called. She found it no surprise that she was deeply in love with the most irritating, sexiest man on earth, Detective David Gillard Larkin, super cop extraordinaire.

The problem was not whether he loved her in return. She knew he did. They had loved each other for as long as either of them could remember. The problem was whether he was ready to be exclusive? To love only her. To love David was to court a broken heart, but she could fight against it no longer. She wondered if she would confess it to him tonight, or would he confess it to her first?

She heard a car drive up and expected the promised visit from David. Perhaps it was time for the two of them to have a serious talk. She couldn't stay in this type of limbo any longer. It was becoming too painful, his kisses too intense.

She didn't turn around when she heard the rustle in the plants beside the sidewalk.

"Hi, you get everything cleaned up?"

She felt him squeeze her shoulder hard and turned around in surprise.

"Gordon! My God! Will you never understand that we are not together anymore? What will it take for you to understand?" She felt an unease creep into her consciousness. His face was grim and the grip on her shoulder tightened.

"You are hurting me, Gordon. Let me go."

He only increased the pressure until she cried out.

"I've waited long enough for you to come to your senses, Cheryl," he said between clenched teeth. "Now it's time I took matters into my own hands. You are going to come with me." He grabbed her arm with one hand, sliding his other arm around her shoulders.

When he dragged her up, she tripped and scraped her leg against the concrete bench, half-falling to her knees. She cried out, and he jerked on her arm painfully.

"Cut it out. You don't want me to have to hurt you, do you?" He reached into his pocket and pulled out nylon handcuffs.

Panic clouded her senses but she fought him for all she was worth. He was no weakling, but she was full of adrenalin and strong from her outdoor work. She managed to kick him between his legs and when he doubled over, she ran into the house. He pushed the door open before she could get the lock engaged. He tried to slap her, but she twisted away and ran into the bathroom managing to lock the door. She screamed for all she was worth, trying to open the window so she could be heard. The nightmare continued with Gordon pounding on the door and threatening to punish her if she didn't open up.

"Awk! Naughty boy!"

Cheryl could hear the parrot squawking loudly from the front room. The noise must be upsetting the bird. She looked around for some kind of weapon and could only find hair spray.

The door crashed open.

Gordon reached for her, his eyes bulging, his furious face red, almost purple.

She sprayed him full in the face and ducked underneath his arms when he yelped and rubbed his eyes. Then she ran for the backyard and straight into David the Hero's arms.

"Honey! What a greeting. To what do I owe this pleasure?"

Cheryl wrapped her arms around his large bulk and burrowed her face into his chest.

David set her aside when Gordon came rushing out yelling for her to come back.

She backed up and watched as David grappled with Gordon, who eventually collapsed on the grass still muttering threats. Had he totally lost his mind?

Cheryl sat on David's lap to the immense satisfaction of them both.

"We could chop down the hedge," David said. "Or you could move in with me and we could make this house all shop?"

"David, my work means a lot to me. You do understand that, don't you?" She had her head on his shoulder, and he kissed her cheek.

"Yep. I do. Perhaps if I hadn't seen you at work I might have been a little dense about it. But I was privileged to see you turning that wasteland into a beautiful park. Too bad those folks won't get to use it anymore. You're very good, honey. You love what you do and I do understand that. I love my work too."

"David, one more thing. I don't share. If you aren't

ready to commit, we could just date occasionally, but once we decide to be together, I don't share."

"Ah, again we are in complete agreement. I don't intend to share you with anyone either. I am fully committed, Cher. I know it's taken me a long time to come to the point, but I'm here now. I love you." Quiet reigned, except for a murmur or two while David sealed their bargain.

"Poor Gordon. He really lost it, didn't he?" Cheryl said between kisses.

David held her firmly, both arms wrapped securely around her. Her comfort seemed to depend on those strong arms. What a night it had been!

"Well, I think I understand his problem. I might lose it too if I lost you. I love you, little girl from next door. I've loved you for at least half my life. After all, you're the only one who knows my middle name."

"But no more houses in the apple tree, okay?"

"Okay."

The End, or perhaps a beginning.

CPSIA information can be obtained
at www.ICGtesting.com
Printed in the USA
FFOW04n0320200716
25980FF

9 781682 911679